HOWDY, BOYS

Raider said, "Folks here in town talk about the Claggetts like they're some kind of bad hombres. Me, I never heard of 'em."

Doc said, "So?"

"So, they can't be such great shakes—"

Gunfire. The Claggetts stampeded into the saloon and started blasting at the marshal and his deputies, who returned the fire.

Doc and Raider took cover, Raider taking his bottle with him. A shot shattered it.

He cried, "You clumsy bastards! Watch where the hell you're shootin'!"

J.D. HARDIN

THE SWINDLER'S TRAIL

BERKLEY BOOKS, NEW YORK

THE SWINDLER'S TRAIL

A Berkley Book / published by arrangement with the author

PRINTING HISTORY
Berkley edition / January 1987

ISBN: 0-425-09480-4

A BERKLEY BOOK ® TM 757,375
Berkley Books are published by The Berkley Publishing Group,
200 Madison Avenue, New York, NY 10016.
The name "BERKLEY" and the stylized "B" with design are
trademarks belonging to Berkley Publishing Corporation.

CHAPTER ONE

The rain had been falling in sheets for over thirteen hours when it let up; the sun broke through the sullen overcast, setting the landscape glistening, and twenty minutes later vanished. Once more the gunmetal clouds opened and spilled; rain rattled down on Raider and Doc and their horses and deepened the quagmire that had displaced the road. The downpour drummed on Raider's Stetson, cudgeled his shoulders, battered his back, and sent its dampness through his poncho, his shirt, sweat, and skin. Inside it crawled into his bloodstream and made its way through to the innermost crevices and corners; it flooded his heart; it reduced his brain to a sponge, absorbing and holding the dank. It besotted his soul.

"Christ Almighty, you'd think if it stopped it'd stop and not stop just long enough to catch its breath before startin' up again. Whoever's in charge o' the plumbin' upstairs is doin' a lousy job. Don't they know it's not supposed to rain in southern California this time o' year?"

1

"Doesn't who?" asked Doc, sloughing along beside him.

"Whoever's in charge. What's the matter, can't you hear?"

"Nobody's in charge, Rade. Weather, foul or fair, is a result of the positions and continuity of the fronts and air masses—"

"Oh, shut up!"

"If it's any consolation, Elmo Utterby is in the same boat."

"Who cares? He deserves to be; we don't. Any son of a bitch who'd steal ninety thousand bucks from the company that gives him a job and pay and all oughta be caught in a damn blizzard and froze to death!"

"How far have we come?"

"More'n four hundred miles."

"How far to Mortality?"

"Six thousand."

"Seriously."

"Who the hell cares? We don' even know he's headin' there. He could be on his way to El Paso. Venazoola. Any-wheres."

"Mr. Hollenbeck went through his desk after he lit out. Elmo's a doodler. He must have written the name Belinda fifty times on his pad. Hollenbeck found a week-old copy of the Tombstone *Epitaph* with the article about the Belinda silver strike outside of Mortality in Conconino County circled with red pencil. Utterby is not a professional; he no doubt completely forgot he left such obvious clues behind."

"Or did it on purpose to throw us off his real track."

"I can't believe that. We've already confirmed he passed through Little Lake and Baker. He's definitely heading toward Arizona, which means Conconino County. You said so yourself."

"What he looks to be doing and what he's really doing could be two different things, you know. They could. He coulda already turned north for Montana, for Chrissakes."

"No."

"Yes."

"No! He's heading straight for Mortality. He's not your run-of-the-mill thief who steals and spends: he's a financial expert; he knows money and investments like you know guns and horses. How else could he rise to the position of chief paymaster of the Southern Pacific in only two short years? Hollenbeck called him a financial genius. Rade, he's not heading for Mexico to blow it all on tequila and cantina girls, he intends to use it as bedrock money on which to build a financial empire. He's that kind of a dreamer, Hollenbeck said he was."

"Whatever he's doin', why didn't he take the goddamn train?"

"You despise trains."

"I despise this weather even more."

"Beggars can't be choosers. He had nearly a four-hour start on us. It was blind luck we were able to track him through Little Lake and Baker. How far to the Grand Canyon?"

"Less than a hundred miles. He'll have to skirt it, most likely to the south."

"How would you go?"

"Cut south of the Black Canyon and Pyramid Canyon, cross the Colorado east of Mohave, head for Kingman. He could catch a train there, you know."

"Oh, Lord."

"Santa Fe and Pacific. Take him all the way to Williams. He could switch over there to a northern Santa Fe and Canyon train."

"You think he might?"

"How the hell do I know? You think I'm ridin' inside the son of a bitch's head? What a dumb question!"

"It was. How far from Kingman to Williams?"

"I don't know, the tracks twist and turn through the mountains; figure a hundred forty, fifty miles. From Williams to Mortality's nothin', twenty miles tops. He could walk it. You think maybe we should switch over to the train in Kingman too? I don't know."

"Why not?"

Raider unleashed a litany of negatives, culminating with the assertion that Elmo Utterby "maybe, just maybe could be suckin' us into boardin' the train, then runnin' off in any direction."

He went on, "That newspaper with the red pencil and the doodling Belinda could still be a plant, you know. It could, you know."

The wind arrived, seizing the deluge in its fist and hurling it horizontally, smashing them both full in their faces.

Raider choked, sputtered, cursed, grimaced, and growled. "I'm comin' down with the pneumonia, I know I am. I feel it crawlin' round inside me. By the time we get there they'll have to carry me into the damn hotel on a board. I've never yet met this skunk and already I hate him. How much exactly did he steal?"

"Ninety-three thousand."

"Disgustin'! Pneumonia or not, when we catch up with him I'm gonna bust him up so we'll be able to carry him back in two saddlebags."

"Hollenbeck mentioned he's six foot and weighs one ninety and is in superb physical condition. He's also captain of the Y.M.C.A. boxing team."

"Oh. Well, he sure as hell better be able to handle a gun."

"And he's an expert shot with pistol and rifle."

Raider said nothing. He bowed his head as the storm attacked with renewed fury.

CHAPTER TWO

Mortality, like a thousand other western towns, was clearly suffering growing pains. It had mushroomed overnight with the discovery of silver nearby. Treasure seekers had come running, and trailing them came the parasites and the decent elements: honest businessmen, clergymen, builders, and others. As rapidly as buildings went up, construction still lagged well behind the swelling population.

"We got four times as many folks as we could put up comfortably," asserted the man in charge of the Arizona Livery Stable.

He was tall, ungainly, and aged well beyond his approximately forty years by the relentless Arizona sun. His skin appeared cracked from lack of moisture; his teeth were rotted from neglect; his eyes were bloody from drink—which also, surmised the two Pinkertons, set his hands trembling as he took hold of their reins.

"How's the Belinda doing?" Doc asked.

"Booming like all get out. Biggest bonanza in the territory ever, maybe the biggest in the whole Southwest. Veins six feet wide, solid silver in every direction. Town's gone crazy. I got ten shares in the company. I could be a rich man in two weeks. If you're looking for a hotel, try the Macomber Lodging House. It's the biggest, so it's your best chance of getting any kind of room."

Doc got out his wallet, paid for their horses' keep, and showed him a somewhat blurred photograph of Elmo Utterby.

"Can't say as I recognize him. He wanted? You marshals?"

"Relatives," said Raider. "His wife sent us out after him."

"Sure." The man smiled his brown and yellow smile and winked broadly. "And I'm Rutherford B. Hayes. Whatever he's done, I don't know him. Macomber's just up the street. Big sign over the door, rockers on the veranda. My nephew's the manager. Ask for Cleon Phelps, that's him."

The Macomber Lodging House was six doors up the street, but no sooner did they spot it then their attention was drawn farther up the way on the opposite side. Doc hastily fumbled Elmo Utterby's picture out of his wallet a second time.

"It's him, Rade, going into that hotel. Let's go."

"Let's not. It's him, it sure looks like him, but he's surer than hell not goin' anyplace. He's either checkin' in or has already. No bag, he musta checked in. Leave him be, let's go clean out the damps. I'm thirsty as hell. Besides, I need a drink for medicinal purposes to knock out the pneumonia."

As if to confirm pneumonia's arrival, he sniffled noisily. Doc watched Utterby enter the hotel and ran ahead a few steps, reaching an angle that permitted him to read the sign over the door.

"American Hotel. What are you talking about, drink? Why drag it out? I say we collar him right now."

"He's not goin' anyplace."

"Wrap it up first, then relax."

"You wrap it up, I'm goin' and get me a splash."

Off he trudged, still soaking wet, despite the sun's re-emergence an hour earlier. Doc took a last look at the American, threw up his hands, and followed. He could hardly argue. Having arrived, Utterby certainly wouldn't be leaving. Not today. He had come to Mortality to do business and was not likely to leave until he'd completed it.

Seated in the Crystal Palace Saloon with a bottle of whiskey between them, they deliberately fell silent, the better to overhear the conversations around them.

"The Belinda strike is the biggest since the Comstock Lode."

"Bigger, and it's making Mortality bigger'n Virginia City."

"Half the population o' Arizona'll wind up millionaires, you watch."

"I wish to hell one thing, I wish to hell the marshal and his deputies was up to handling them Claggetts. Mark my words, those boys are out to spill blood, anybody's to get a rope around this town. And with it the Belinda."

"There's no way under the sun they can, Edward. The Big Bonanza Company's got complete, absolute control over the diggings. The bank's the sole agent for the stock; Eustace Atherton, the president, is controller and disbursing commissioner. Not a share gets bought or sold without his say-so and okay. There's nothing the Claggetts or anybody else can do to rewire the setup."

"They can raise hell high enough to take over the town. They can wipe out law and order and be in the driver's seat. Then walk into the bank and divide Eustace Atherton into little pieces."

"Tell you what we oughta do, every man jack of us. Posse us together a vigilante group, ride out to the Claggetts, round 'em up like steers, and run 'em outta Conconino County."

"That's big talk, but count me outta tryin' it. That scum got more blood on their hands than a slaughterhouse catch basin. I ain't about to add mine to it."

"Amen to that, Edward."

Raider sipped. "What the hell's goin' on around here do you think?"

"You heard. It doesn't surprise me. Wherever there's a big strike there's a struggle for control, for power. One goes with the other. When Harry Comstock swindled the two Irishmen out of the Washoe Diggings all hell could have broken loose if they'd had a few guns to back them up. How in the world Comstock ever got away with it is the mystery of the age. Had these Claggetts been there..."

Raider lowered his head. "The way these boys talk they got to be worse than the James boys and Youngers rolled into one. Myself, I never heard of 'em."

"So?"

"They can't be such big shakes."

A gun went off. The scantily clad odalisque stretched out seductively in her gilded frame over the bar mirror took the slug an inch above her left eye. Chairs scraped the floor, the piano slammed shut, feet scrambled, poker chips spilled and scattered, bottles upended, liquor sloshed, voices cried out in fearful tones. Two more shots followed. Four men bearing a distinct family likeness, all with pug noses, beady eyes, pugnacious chins, and prominent ears, all dirty-looking in dusty clothes and well-worn boots and hats, came stampeding through the batwing doors. At the same time a heavyset man sporting a marshal's tin and wielding two .45s rushed in through the back door followed by a string of badged deputies. Between sips the two Pinkertons were magically whisked from a noisy saloon to a battlefield, seated squarely between the two sides.

When the other patrons hit the floor they followed suit, Raider grabbing the bottle as he went down. He struck his nose. "Ow!"

"Clumsy! Pass the bottle."

Shots whirred over their heads. The marshal and his men had turned tables up on their edges, erecting a makeshift barrier. Doc could see lead chewing and whitening the tops. A man bellowed behind him and fell so hard he rattled the floor under them both.

"I hit my nose."

"The bottle, " rasped Doc.

"How in hell can you drink at a time like this?"

"It's times like these I need a drink!"

Doc reached for it. Raider pushed it to within an inch of his grasp. A shot shattered it. He jerked his hand back.

"Son of a bitch! Paid for and everythin'. You clumsy bastards! Watch where the hell you're shootin'!"

Two shots pushed his head down. He struck his nose a second time. "Goddamn!"

"Shut your mouth and freeze," ordered Doc.

His command seemed to reach all ears save those of the combatants. Not a patron stirred, not an eye sneaked a peek, everyone held his breath. On raged the hostilities. Two more brothers had come in on the heels of the first four. Now two backed out, taking up positions at the corners of the front window and blasting at the law through the glass. It took a number of holes before shattering loudly and completely, whereupon the bartender came up from behind his mahogany with a twelve-gauge and emptied both barrels at the parties responsible at the corners outside. Smoking gun in hand, he surveyed the results of his effort. It was the last mistake he would ever make; one of the four brothers inside threw two shots at him, shattering one cheek and drilling his eye. Down he went, down crashed the mirror on top of him, down fell the odalisque, hanging upside down by one corner out of sight on a misplaced nail.

The four brothers inside, crouching behind tables themselves, began to withdraw, pulling their cover with them back to the doors and retreating into the street. Behind them they left one dead and one badly wounded, the youngest among them having taken a slug in the shoulder and another deep in his hip. They made no effort to pull him along with them.

Blue smoke still hung in the air, and the stink of cordite lingered when the marshal and his men finally rose and emerged from behind their cover. One deputy lay dead with a hole in his forehead; another nursed a badly shattered hand gloved crimson. Seven patrons had suffered a variety of wounds, ranging from the two shot in the heart and instantly killed to one elderly man who loudly complained of the loss of his right earlobe.

Raider and Doc emerged from the fray badly shaken but unscathed, apart from Raider's aching nose.

"Jesus Christ," he rasped, "if this doesn't beat all. We're not in town fifteen minutes and we're nearly killed, and without gettin' a shot off, without even gettin' to see what's goin' on, without even knowin' anybody who's doin' the goin' on. You sure know how to pick a table, Weatherbee, smack in the middle."

"It was the only one available, friend."

"This oughta tell you why."

"Funny."

The five corpses were carried out, a doctor was sent for, and the wounded were treated. The captured Claggett was attended to and taken away to jail. Outrage overflowed the banks of the patrons' fear. They crowded around the marshal.

"How in hell can you let something like this happen, Evan!" burst out a fat, sweating mountain of a man, his face pale as a sheet.

"Easy, boys, we didn't *let* anything happen, it just did. We spotted the Claggetts coming in and did the only thing we could—try and get the drop on them and stop the shooting before they could open up. We got here a tad late."

"I guess to hell you did!" boomed his accuser. Others grumbled agreement.

The marshal was being surprisingly patient with the fault-finders. He was obviously doing his best to control the Claggetts; an indoor shoot-out involving innocent bystanders, two of whom had been killed, was not of his choosing. He seemed to be damned if he engaged the Claggetts and damned if he didn't. Why he didn't rip his badge off and hurl it in the fat man's carping and sneering face was more than Doc could fathom.

"These people don't deserve a decent marshal, a man who's not afraid to use his guns," he said. "Let's get out of here."

Outside, they surveyed the shattered front window. From the sidewalk the interior looked as if a tornado had passed through. The surviving Claggetts were by now miles away. Marshal Evan Rhilander still stood patiently absorbing the complaints and criticism of the innocents. One of his men came out reloading his Peacemaker. His face was that of one who had forgotten to lock his doors upon leaving home. Worry seamed his brow, his dark eyes overflowed with it, and the corners of his mouth drooped with disappointment under his gray cheeks.

"What a mess," he said to Raider and Doc. He stared. "You boys new in town?"

They introduced themselves as Martin Blaisdell, Doc's usual alias, and Mr. O'Toole, Raider's. The deputy's name was Mason Rodwell.

"They're dead set on taking over the town," he explained. "They haven't a chance in hell, of course, but they think they do, and in the meantime blood gets spilled. You boys might be wise to do your drinking in your hotel room."

"Oh boy!" Doc snapped his fingers. He grabbed Raider by the arm, touched the brim of his curly-brim derby to Rodwell, and hurried his partner away.

"What the hell's bitin' you?"

"Aren't you forgetting something?"

"Utterby's not goin' anyplace. He's likely still upstairs nappin' off the miles. An' smarter than we were, bringin' his bottle up with him like the deputy said."

"We never should have gone near that place," lamented Doc. "I should never listen to you. Apart from nearly getting our heads blown off, it's given him all kinds of time."

"To do what, for Chrissakes! Doc, will you stop bein' such a' old lady? I keep tellin' you he's here to stay. For a time, for sure. Hey, you hear what that fella said his name was, Mason Rodwell? He's an ex-hired gun gone straight.

I heard about him up in Montana. He rustled and turned over banks, hit Wells Fargo for a bundle, then got religion and reformed himself. Isn't that nice?"

"Keep moving. You can talk and walk at the same time."

"That's nice. His mother must be real pleased."

They reached the American Hotel. Doc raced up the steps and inside, Raider trailing behind, deliberately lagging. The lobby was typical, redolent of stogie smoke, decorated with two scruffy-looking potted palms battling to survive on a diet of tobacco ashes and cigar stubs. The desk clerk was immersed in a book covered with butcher's paper, concealing both title and author. It must have been a joke book; he tittered, giggled, laughed, or hooted loudly every few lines. Doc requested his attention. Raider came up, slammed the desk bell, and got it.

"What's the matter, what!" exclaimed the startled clerk.

Doc showed Utterby's picture. The clerk squinted, frowned, adjusted his spectacles, took a second long look, pursed his thin lips, scratched his head, pondered. . . .

"Do you know him or don'cha!" snapped Raider.

"Never seen him before in my life, but I just come on ten minutes ago. He could have checked in before——"

Steps. Someone was descending the stairs. She appeared in scarlet flounces, glittering sequins, a hat with lightly bouncing ostrich feathers, and carrying a parasol, a large alligator gladstone bag, and a reticule. She had not spared the makeup, but it was artfully applied and in good taste. She turned a pair of smoldering brown eyes on Raider as she glided past. He withered under their assault, swallowing, turning and watching her disappear through the double doors.

"Wow! Was that a woman or was that a woman!"

The clerk was still studying Utterby's picture. "Does this photo have a name?"

"Abe Lincoln," rasped Raider. "If you don't know who he is and you've never seen him, what do you care?"

"His name is Elmo Utterby," said Doc patiently, glaring at his partner. "He's no doubt using an alias, but would you please check the register anyway?"

The clerk did so. There was no Elmo Utterby.

"Let's see," said Raider, grabbing the book and turning it around. "Look at the different handwritin's, Doc, uh, Martin. You saw his doodling pad back at the office, look."

Doc sighed defeatedly but obliged him. He shook his head. "I can't possibly tell. He signed a phony name. He must have taken pains to disguise his handwriting as well."

"You boys like a room?"

"We're goin' to the Macomber," said Raider.

"You have one available?" Doc asked.

"A lovely corner room. The party just checked out when I came on."

"We'll take it."

"Doc . . . Martin."

Doc signed the register. Key in hand, he mounted the stairs to the second floor, Raider dallying behind.

"What are you doin' this for?"

"We both saw Utterby come into this place. It was him, no mistake. If you hadn't insisted on dragging me to the nearest saloon we could have followed and taken him. I can't believe he'd enter and register, then leave and go elsewhere. It doesn't make sense."

"It does if he figured he's bein' followed, and there's no way he can't figure that."

"We're still better off here than at the Macomber House. If he does think he's being followed, he'll hardly resort to changing hotels. He knows he'd be wasting his time. Keep in mind, Rade, he's an intelligent man, an amateur embezzler, perhaps, but with brains. My guess is he's figured his plan out to a nicety, every piece in place, every alternative and angle considered."

They stopped before 2B. Doc thrust the key into the hole and paused.

"Go downstairs and ask the desk clerk when the man he relieved is coming back on. Better yet, find out where he lives and we'll go see him."

"Doc . . ."

"Just do it, Rade, please. We wouldn't be in this fix if we'd followed him in."

"Are you gonna throw that at me till the Last Judgment? Are you? If you are, you better not, I mean it."

"Go. Here, take Utterby's picture."

"Okay, okay."

The early duty clerk recalled Elmo Utterby registering the instant he saw his picture. Only he'd signed in as George Watson of Kansas City. Raider rejoined Doc at the American House and together they pressed the joke book reader for Watson's room number.

The clerk's narrowed eyes shifted from one to the other and back. "What do you want him for?" He looked as if he suspected them of trying to pick his pocket.

"He's wanted in Sacramento for wife beating," said Raider airily.

Doc flung his eyes at the ceiling, but said nothing.

"And who are you?"

"Detectives. This here is Detective Blaisdell and I'm Detective O'Toole."

"You have some kind of identification?"

"What do you want with that?"

"To see if you're who you say you are."

"He's Operative Raider, I'm Operative Weatherbee," said Doc in a defeated tone. "We're with the Pinkerton National Detective Agency."

"He just said—"

"Never mind!" interrupted Raider.

They showed their ID's.

"Room six B, right down the hall from your room."

Doc nodded. "Thank you, and this is confidential, okay? You don't know what we are, who we're with."

"And I don't care."

The door to 6B was locked. The clerk refused to let them in with his passkey; he denied he even had one.

"I know the law. When a guest's not in his or her room

you have to get a court order to enter, if you don't work for the hotel, that is."

"Fella," said Raider, "if you don't let us in there, and right now, you'll be in the hottest water north o' hell itself. This boy's a wanted criminal in the first degree. He's a murderer, a horse thief, a money thief, and six other crimes. Now, are you gonna let us in there or do we call Marshal Rhilander, get him over here, and have him toss you in the clink for obstructin' justice and aidin' and abettin' a known wanted criminal? What'll it be?"

To Doc's surprise and Raider's dismay the room showed not a single sign of occupancy. It was as neat as a pin, the bed made, every article in its proper place, no suitcase or bag, the closet empty.

"I'll be damned," groused Raider. "Son of a bitch has hornswoggled us for fair. You sure this is his room?"

"Six B," said the clerk. His grin cut straight through Raider's glower.

"Do you know if he's been going in and out?" asked Doc. "No, you couldn't know that. I guess that does it. Let's go, Rade."

"Where?"

"Back to see the other man. Lead the way."

The early duty clerk doubled as a counterman at Principe's General Merchandise Mart. He stood behind his bib apron, his hair slicked down like leather on either side of his part. "You find Mr. Watson?" he asked.

"He flew the coop," Raider answered. "Did he go in and out much after he signed in?"

Doc laid a hand on Raider's forearm. "About what time did he register?"

"I'd say around eleven this morning."

"We didn't get here till after three," Doc said to Raider.

"I didn't pay attention to his comings and goings. No need, you know? I mean, it's the guest's business."

"You're sure he didn't check out," said Doc.

"Not while I was on. I got off at four."

"He didn't check out after," said Raider. "The boy with the joke book would have said."

Doc's glum look said it all. "He's apparently vanished into thin air."

"The hell he has, he's lit out is what he's done."

"I disagree. Why come all this way to stay only a couple of hours?"

"Like I said, he's afraid he's bein' followed."

"He *knows* he is, knows he's leading us here. He's obviously planned accordingly."

They thanked the man behind the counter and wandered outside. The sun blazed. Not a puddle could be seen in the street; the horse troughs were filled to capacity. They stood next to a tall, precariously piled pillar of tin washtubs. A heaping, steaming, stinking load of manure trundled by. Raider stared; it seemed to characterize the state of affairs as of the moment.

"He's playin' with us, Doc."

"So it seems."

"One thing, it could be he didn't check out deliberate, just left without sayin'."

"Possibly."

"My head's startin' to spin. I gotta get somethin' to eat. I can't think on a empty stomach."

After she left the American Hotel, the lady in red set her course for the Mortality Miners & Merchants Bank. Greeted by a teller, she politely asked to see President Eustace Atherton. The teller left her to pose and survey the bank, and moments later a ruddy-faced, neckless, dapper-looking gentleman shaped quite like a potbellied stove smiled benignly and beckoned her into his office.

It reeked of bay rum, as did its occupant. Gesturing his visitor to a chair, he introduced himself. She sat with both hands perched on the upended handle of her parasol, beaming graciously. She cleared her throat in a ladylike fashion, touching her throat as she did so, then let her fingers float upward to her hair for a touch there.

"Delighted to meet you. I am Agatha Witherspoon, the widow Witherspoon."

"Ah, my sincere condolences, madam."

"I won't take much of your time."

"You're welcome to as much as you require."

She opened her capacious alligator gladstone bag. "I have with me a considerable sum of money which I would like to invest in the Big Bonanza Company Limited."

Atherton's eyes gleamed like a sidewinder's studying a baby gopher. The tip of his tongue rode his ample upper lip full length.

"Ninety thousand dollars," said his visitor.

His eyes bulged briefly and his florid features took on the look of one who had just found gold in his washbasin.

"Ninety thousand..." His shock vanished and he flew into action, uncapping his fountain pen, slapping a pad on his blotter, and readying to write. "You're very fortunate. I'm happy to say the stock is available and the price today is holding at yesterday's price. Fifty dollars per share for premium, thirty-eight for common."

"Premium."

"Ah, that will be..." He began scribbling. "Eighteen hundred shares."

She drew from her bag four large banded packets of bills, setting them neatly side by side before him.

"Ah, pray excuse me." Wetting his thumb, he deftly counted each stack. Still propped on her parasol, she watched him with a look of forbearance that seemed to gradually slip into outright boredom. The odor of bay rum continued to assault their nostrils. The soft rippling of the bills under his thumb steadied and continued as he whispered occasional subtotals. And the sun outside his window lowered over the distant Aubrey Cliffs.

"Ninety thousand to the penny. Eighteen hundred premium shares. My dear Mrs. Witherspoon, you have just made yourself the investment of a lifetime. You have just, may I say it, made your fortune. You have—"

"Forgive me, but I'm in a bit of a rush."

"Of course, of course. We'll be done in a jiffy. If you'll be so kind, wait right where you are and I'll go to the vault and get your certificates. Unless, of course, you prefer that the bank hold them for you."

"I'll hold them, thank you."

"As you wish. I'll just be a shake. Ah, while you're waiting, would you care for a French bonbon?"

"No, thank you."

"A chocolate covered pecan? They're my favorite."

"Just the certificates, thank you."

"Of course." Off he sprinted.

Raider and Doc stood under the Merchandise Mart overhang directly opposite the bank. Doc was preparing to speak when a furor erupted at the far end of the street. There was shouting, shooting, and five horses came galloping toward them. Five horses bearing only four riders. The fleeing men wheeled left and vanished into an alley.

A boy came rushing up the middle of the street, his straw hat flying from his head, his hand cupped around his mouth. "It's the Claggetts, the Claggetts! Tried to bust into the jail and get back Elon. He's been shot again! The marshal, too! The Claggetts, the Claggetts!"

Raider and Doc exchanged glances.

"Elon," murmured Doc, "must be the one wounded in the Crystal Palace shoot-out."

Raider shook his head and sucked his back teeth on one side. "What a setup. Even when they catch 'em they can't hang 'em without a fight. Oh well, it's no skin off our hides."

"It is if they get in the way of our job," rasped Doc. "We've got our hands full as it is."

"Throwin' it in my face again, aren't you?"

"I merely said—"

"He's still here, he's got to be."

"Where? Tell me."

"In town, in town. Whatta ya gettin' all steamed up for?"

Mason Rodwell and three deputies appeared, thundering up the street and wheeling into the alley in pursuit. Raider's glance shifted to the bank. The door opened and out floated the lady in red, still carrying her bag and reticule.

"Hey, there she is again, Doc. Is that a woman or is that a woman? Wow!"

"Sssh, for heaven sakes."

"Will ya look at that balcony. Great day, if she ain't an eyeful for fair!"

She took no notice of them. Turning left, she set off down the street, passing a pair of loungers seated in front of the Arizona Livery Stable, drawing their admiring eyes after her, setting one whistling and slapping his knee. A well-dressed older gentleman coming the other way passed her, paused, turned, and looked back, ogling her up and down over his pinch glasses.

"She's goin' into the restaurant. C'mon, Doc."

"What do you think you're doing?"

"I tol' ya I'm hungry. Starvin', in fact. C'mon, let's haul on the feed bag."

Raider went out of his way to select a table diagonally opposite that of the lady in red. Between them stood an unoccupied table for two.

"Rade, behave yourself. I mean it. We're here to eat, not for you to make a spectacle of yourself."

"Sssssh! I'm not doin' nothing. Just lookin'. Don't hurt nothin' to look. Hey, did you see that?"

"What?"

"She smiled at me. She recognizes me from the lobby, you betcha. Hot dog!"

"Will you cut it out! You're behaving like a lovesick schoolboy."

The waiter appeared with his menus under his arm, his

pad and pencil in hand. They ordered steaks—Doc's rare; Raider's "bloody, warm, and tender as a girl baby's kiss." No sooner did their meals arrive then a woman of enormous, even elephantine, proportions, from her casklike head atop her five-stack chins to her size 14 beaver button leather fox shoes, rolled into view. Doc reacted mildly to the sight of her, causing Raider to turn for a look.

"Holy Hannah, will you look at the gas balloon in skirts."

"Rade . . ."

"She's gonna bust the floor for sure. Hang on to your hats, folks. If this was a ship we'd be headin' for the bottom!"

She had passed by the potted fern at the entrance, obliterating it from sight, and was directing her bulk toward the empty table squarely between Raider and the object of his attention.

"Oh no! Oh for Chrissakes!"

"Rade, will you stop it!"

"Look at that, she's sittin' down right in the damn way. She is. She . . . oh for . . ."

He had seized the edge of the table and was rocking from side to side and jumping up and down as if invisible strings attached to him were being manipulated by spastic hands. Everyone stared.

"Sit down!"

"If that don't beat all, son of a . . ." He sank slowly into his chair, completely and utterly defeated.

"Eat."

The new arrival angled her huge head coquettishly, poked a chubby forefinger under her nethermost chin, beamed girlishly at Raider, and winked. He growled behind an expression of pure disdain. She reacted with shock, then hurt. The waiter approached. She accepted a menu from him and hid her face behind it.

They finished their coffee, paid the bill, and left, all without so much as a single syllable of additional conversation. Raider lagged behind as they each appropriated a toothpick by the door and went out.

"Let's go, Rade."

Raider had turned around and was backing out. "She's having her coffee. She's eatin' one o' those little nut and cream cakes with the cherry on top for dessert. Looks tasty. Whatta you say we go back and have us a couple? At another table. The one right across from hers is free now."

"Let's not. We've got work to do. I've got an idea. If we can't find Elmo right off the bat, I think we can at least protect ourselves against losing him."

"That makes a lotta sense."

"Move."

CHAPTER THREE

Doc's idea made sense enough to pursue. They made the rounds, showing Utterby's photograph to the Wells Fargo agent and the managers of all three livery stables. It was at the last of these—"Hunnicutt's Horses and Vehicles for Hire and Storage, for Sale, Exchange, and Rent, by the Hour, Day, Week, or Month"—that they got lucky. Arris Hunnicutt took one look at the picture and nodded. He scratched his grizzled chin, ran a bony finger under his nose, sniffled, spat, shifted his weight from one foot to the other, and spoke.

"That'sss him. Come in thisss morning."

"Riding a big chestnut gelding," said Raider, a fact established on their way to Mortality when his picture was recognized in Little Lake and Baker.

"That he wasss. It'sss right back there in the corner ssstall. What'sss he done you want him for?"

"Believe it or not, Mr. Hunnicutt, Mr. . . . ."

"Watsssson. Leassstwisse that'sss what he called himsssself to me."

"He's inherited a considerable sum, and we'd like to catch up with him and tell him the good news."

"Believe it or not, did you sssay? Not. On sssecond thought I don't muchly care what you want him for, I ain't Nosssy Parker; got busss'ness enough of my own to tend to. Where he isss now I can't sssay. He can't have left town, though, not and leave his horssse behind."

"We're staying at the American," said Doc. "If he does come back to pick up his horse, would you mind letting us know? If we don't happen to be in, just leave word at the desk."

"Gladly, how much isss he worth to you?"

"Two bits," said Raider.

"Five dollars," said Doc, "and our appreciation."

"You got a deal."

They thanked him and walked off.

"Two bits," scoffed Doc. "Will you ever learn?"

"Oh, horseshit. If you mean will I ever learn to throw money around like so much hen feed like some people I know, the answer is hell no. I start small and work my way up, but only if I got to. That's the smart way to haggle. What now?"

"Let's try the bank."

"What for?"

"Humor me. I want to see if I guessed right, that he came here to invest in the Belinda. If that was his intention he's had more than enough time to do it."

It was past six o'clock and the bank was shuttered for the night. They went around back in hopes that President Atherton or one of his employees might be working late, but they had no luck. The back door was locked.

"What do you think?" Doc asked. "Should we go see the marshal and ring him in? It couldn't hurt."

"I don't see it can help none. Too many cooks spoil the soup, you know. Besides, he got himself shot up in that squabble this afternoon. He's prob'ly in no shape to help himself to the outhouse, let alone us."

There was little left for them to do but mosey about town

in hopes of accidentally bumping into Utterby. As it happened, over the course of the ensuing three hours they did so no fewer than four separate times. All four times the lady in red accorded Raider the same beaming, seductive smile. By the time they called it a night and started back to the hotel he was bursting with frustration.

Little did either he or Doc suspect that the fourth time they crossed paths with the lady was to be the last time ever.

Eustace Atherton offered them French bonbons, fancy mixed candy in a five-pound tin, caramels, and princess squares with assorted colored tops. It was not hard to see where the man's corpulence came from.

"Ninety-three thousand, you say?" Atherton whistled softly, rose from his chair, and, moving to the closed door, locked it. "Quite a tidy sum."

"We think he came to Mortality to invest in the Belinda."

"If he did I haven't seen him in here. And if that was his intention he'd have to come to us. We're sole agents for the company."

"He'd have to deal directly with you."

"Absolutely. I hold sole authorization for the sale of both the premium and common stock. By the way, if you boys are interested . . ."

Both shook their heads.

"Did anybody purchase stock yesterday to the value of anywhere near that figure?" Doc asked.

"A lady did."

Doc and Raider exchanged puzzled looks.

"Bought eighteen hundred shares of premium, ninety thousand cash on the barrel head. Set the money out right there on the desk, right between the bonbons and the chocolate-covered pecans I polished off last night. Four stacks of bills."

"Would you describe her?"

Atherton did so. The longer he went on, the more detailed his description, the redder Raider's cheeks became.

"Son of a bitch," he muttered.

Atherton frowned. "I beg your pardon."

"Not you. Nothin'."

Doc could scarcely contain himself. He sat in his chair jiggling and fidgeting so much that one might imagine he was under assault on all sides by feathers. He finally burst into a gale of laughter, roaring, lifting and lowering his upper body, laughing until the tears rolled down his cheeks and his face took on a hue two shades redder than Atherton's normal complexion. "I don't believe it!"

"Will you shut up the dumb caterwaulin'!"

"Did I say something?" asked Atherton innocently.

"No no no no no," responded Doc. "It's nothing, honestly."

"My word, if you don't mind my saying so, how would you react if it was something?"

"It's an inside joke," explained Doc. "I wouldn't want to bore you with the details." Battling back a second bout of laughter with a momentous effort of will, he sobered. "You say she identified herself as . . ."

"Agatha Witherspoon, the widow Witherspoon."

"Priceless. Marvelous! I love it. Did she mention where she was staying?"

"No. And not a word about where she was from, what her business was. Nothing, other than that her husband was dead."

"Did you ask her to sign anything?"

"No, it wasn't necessary. I got the certificates out of the vault, she paid me the money, we shook hands, and that was that. She was carrying an alligator gladstone bag and a reticule. She put the certificates in the bag—there were sixteen in all, each one worth fifty shares. Eighteen hundred. Premium stock, as I said. I remember her bag as quite handsome. With a double hasp lock and side catches. Yes, quite handsome indeed."

"Well, thank you, Mr. Atherton," Doc said. "You've been very helpful."

"Has she done anything wrong? My Lord, she's not a

criminal? The money she gave me wasn't stolen?"

"Not that we know of," lied Doc.

Instinctively sensing that Raider was about to say something, Doc, standing beside him, both having risen from their chairs, pinched him painfully.

"Ouch!"

Atherton stared. "My word."

"It's nothing," explained Doc. "He has an ulcer that kicks up. Well, I guess we'll be on our way, and thank you again."

On the way out the front door, just as Doc finished mildly scolding Raider for nearly spilling the beans, the two had to make way for a doddering old gentleman sporting a full white beard that covered his face to within an inch of his eyes. He walked with the aid of a gold-trimmed Congo cane. Neither took note of him, but he stared furtively at first one then the other.

His eyes twinkled merrily.

CHAPTER FOUR

RE YR INQUIRY RE EU STOP HAVE DEFINITELY ES-
TAB HE WAS ACTIVE LOCAL SEMIPROF ACTING CO
STOP ESSAYED VARIETY ROLES STOP CO MGR
CONFIRMS HE ALSO DOUBLED AS MAKEUP ARTIST
STOP TRUST THIS HELPS STOP URGE UTMOST POS-
SIBLE HASTE TRACKING FUGITIVE DOWN AND RE-
TRIEVING MONEY BEFORE ALL IS SQUANDERED
STOP YOUR PRINCIPAL ASSURES ME YOU ARE HIS
BEST MEN FOR THE JOB SPRS FATE LIES SQUARELY
IN YOUR EXPERT HANDS STOP DONT REPEAT DONT
REPEAT DONT LET US DOWN
      E. S. HOLLENBECK
      PRESIDENT SPR

Raider and Doc stood outside the Western Union Office,
Doc holding the telegram.

"Great, wonderful," he said morosely. "Would you mind
telling me why it is that nobody, I mean nobody we work

27

for, ever stops to consider that we're only human, that it's impossible to solve every case we tackle, and that should we fail to solve it for whatever reason, we're not criminals? Be honest, don't you ever get the feeling that if we mess up we should go to jail for punishment?"

Raider nodded. "I can see the handwritin' on the wall clear as a bell. We blow this one and old A.P.'ll have us drawn and quartered and the Southern Pacific'll prob'ly sue the agency."

"On the grounds of disappointment or something." Doc held up the wire. "Cheer up, this is the confirmation we were looking for."

Raider scoffed. "All the hell it does is confirm how impossible it's gonna be to track the son of a bitch down. Anybody can pass himself off as a female that great, that—"

"Cleverly."

"—might just as well be walkin' around Butte, Montana. We musta seen her, him, it, six times, comin' within a foot o' her more'n twice, and never dreamed it was him. He fooled Atherton, too. He fooled everybody."

"He's good. But even the best disguise can be penetrated."

"Let's go see if we can find him, her."

"We'd only be wasting our time; he has to have changed disguises by now. He'd be an idiot not to, and the one thing he isn't is an idiot. No, Rade, he played the grand lady in red to throw us off the track so he could approach Atherton to buy the stock. He did so, and now you can bet the rent he's switched to another character."

"You think he's still hangin' around town?"

"Why leave? He can disguise himself, but not his horse."

"He can swap it for another."

"But Hunnicutt would know; Utterby knows that. Face it, he's safe as a baby in disguise. Why leave town, why hide in his room, why do anything but carry on in a perfectly normal manner? Bank on it, he's waiting with everybody else around here, including the desk clerk, for the good ship Belinda to come in."

"Which it's already doin'. Lemme see his picture again."

"What for?"

"I just wanta stare at it. Fix it in my head, you know? He can disguise himself, sure, and real good, but certain things he can't change. Like his eyes and the way he holds his head, his walk, lotsa things."

Doc handed him the picture. Raider crinkled his brow and glared at it fiercely. A passing breeze raised twin dust devils in the street, came blowing their way and past them, snatching the picture from his grasp and sending it sailing upward, spinning, whirling, changing directions.

"Hey!"

"Oh for heaven sakes."

They ran after it. Doc almost got a hand on it, but the mischievous culprit jerked it just above his grasp. Then dashed it downward, landing it in the horse trough.

"Oh for Chrissakes."

Doc fished it out with the utmost care. "It's all right, it's all right. We just have to be careful not to tear it. It'll dry out in this heat in fifteen minutes."

"Give it here."

"I'll handle it."

"Give it here, Doc, I know just what to do, drape it over the hitch rack there, only with just the top edge stickin' so's when it dries it won't stick all over and rip to shreds when you try to pull it off. Go ahead, do it. You're sure as hell not gonna stand there with your face hangin' out, holdin' it by one corner for the next fifteen minutes, are you?"

"Anything to please Your Majesty."

Doc carefully affixed one upper corner of the picture to the end of the hitch rack so that the sun beat directly upon it. No sooner did he step back to appraise his handiwork then two shots rang out, the second one skimming the up-turned edge of his curly-brim derby, spinning it from his head. Down he went, flattening against the sidewalk. Down went Raider, flattening against the road, striking his nose on the edge of the sidewalk.

"Owwww!"

A wild flurry of shots, seemingly coming from all directions, followed the first two. Women screamed, men shouted and cursed, horses neighed, pandemonium reigned. Innocent bystanders did not stand by; like Raider and Doc they flattened or jumped for cover or hurled themselves through open windows and doors. Dust kicked up around Raider, bracketing him. Shouts came from both ends of the street, punctuated by spirited gunfire. Attackers and defenders began spreading out, taking cover behind barrels, parked wagons, horse troughs, whatever proved handy.

"Damn nose! What the hell is it with this town? Every time we turn around, somebody's unloadin' against somebody else."

"It must be Claggetts again. Keep your head down."

"If it was any lower, it'd be buried, for Chrissakes! We're right in the line o' fire, Doc. Just like the saloon. Let's catch the lull if we can and make a run for that door there. It's an office or somethin'."

Rifles joined the fray, as well as a single shotgun, its sonorous blast sharply distinct from the other sounds. A shot caught the edge of Raider's heel, ricocheting off it, prompting him to jerk his leg and blue the air with curses. Another shot thudded into the horse trough and two more chewed the stile and the post beside it of the door they planned to flee to.

"These guys are wilder than wet hens," rasped Raider.

Doc had begun bellying toward the door, but the two wild shots froze him some four feet from it.

"The devil with the door," he muttered. "I'm going for the alley. You coming?"

Raider didn't answer; instead he rose to a crouch, moved four steps toward the alley, and threw himself into it, closely followed by a shotgun blast. Doc held his breath, got up on all fours, and scrambled to join him. Their backs flat against the wall, they stood side by side out of the line of fire.

"What the hell did that shotgun shoot at me for, do you think? I mean he aimed—"

"Just another wild shot."

"You lost your hat."

"I'll get it."

"That was no wild shot, Doc, that was Utterby."

"Nonsense."

"No nonsense. He sure knows us by sight, him bein' the lady in red. What better way to get rid of us than under the cover o' somebody else's fracas?"

"You have a vivid imagination."

"Right, that's how come I know."

The battle raged for a few minutes more, then, as abruptly as it began, it stopped. Raider and Doc continued to stand flattened against the wall, neither one willing to chance a look, thereby exposing himself to a tardy final shot. Presently, voices could be heard, wheels rolling, hooves clopping the street. People emerged from their cover, ordinary life and traffic resumed in Mortality.

"Coast is clear," said Raider.

They started toward the sidewalk. Raider in the lead nearly bumped into Mason Rodwell, who was passing by.

"Hello there," he said pleasantly. "You okay?"

Raider grunted.

Doc nodded. "No thanks to the trigger-happy element." He bent and retrieved his derby. And gasped. A bullet had drilled clean through the crown. "Will you look at that."

"Lucky your head wasn't in it," said Rodwell.

"How come all the shootin', Deputy? Seems like every few minutes somebody gets the itch to shoot up the town."

"Not somebody, the Claggetts."

"What on earth do they want?" Doc asked. "Seriously, what do they hope to gain with all the fireworks?"

"Control. Virgil, the oldest one, ran for marshal against Evan Rhilander. Evan beat him by better than three to one. Virgil claimed he rigged the voting, stuffed the boxes. The ballot boxes were impounded. Judge Aletter examined them and rendered his decision, declaring Evan the winner."

"How the hell could a three-to-one wallopin' be rigged?" asked Raider. "Makes no sense at all."

"Chalk it up to a sore loser. The thing of it is, the marshal's the law, and one of his responsibilities, his biggest one, outside of keeping the Claggetts in check, is seeing to it that law and order prevail out at the Belinda. Two deputies are out there full time. Evan is straight as a die, and he'd have the hide of any of his men he caught with their hand in the cookie jar. If Virgil was marshal his hand would be stuck in it permanently. Given the chance, he and his clan would turn the Belinda and the town upside down and catch everything that falls out. They're not only crooked and killers, they're all short of hat size—I mean crazy as bedbugs. All any of 'em know is shoot, shoot, shoot."

"So we see," said Raider dryly.

"Virgil won't stop till he kills Evan; in his twisted brain he thinks he can step in and take over. Crazy. Look at what happened yesterday: after that to-do at the Crystal Palace, they came barreling back into town to spring young Elon. Ended up wounding him and Evan, and the boy's still behind bars."

"How bad is the marshal?"

"Just a scratch, but like I said, Virgil won't quit till he's dead. And the other Claggetts toe Virgil's line. He's head of the family."

"The marshal must sleep with his hand on his gun and one eye wide," said Raider.

"Not really. He's not afraid of him, just annoyed. Mark my words, one of these days he's going to go after his ass in earnest. He'll blow him clear out of Conconino County. It's gotten to be a blood feud. I tell Evan that and he doesn't like to hear it, doesn't like the idea of what you might call reducin' his obligation to protect people to swamp fighting to protect himself."

"It sounds like the Claggetts got half a brain between 'em," observed Raider. "If they had any more they'd toss in the sponge and pull up stakes. I mean if they do kill the marshal, somebody else'll just take his place. They'll be no better off than they are now."

"You're talking sensibly," said Rodwell, "but that's not the way they figure it. If they figure at all."

He was staring at Raider. Doc looked from one to the other. There was a striking similarity in their faces. Both wore flowing mustaches, both boasted high cheekbones, lean, clean-shaven jaws, and dark, piercing eyes. Rodwell was older—gray showed in his tar-black hair, and lines as slender as a spiderweb's radiated from the corners of his eyes.

"Have we met before?" he asked Raider.

"Could be."

The sun rose in the deputy's face. "Montana. You're with the Pinkertons, aren't you?"

"Who says?"

"You are. We crossed paths once. In Denton. Those were my hellion days back then. We pulled a little stunt in Garnell, down near Flatville Creek. We lit out and stopped in Denton to catch our breath. You caught up and came within a whisker of grabbing a couple of us. Are you a Pinkerton too?" he asked Doc. "You must be. What are Pinkertons doing in Mortality?"

"Slummin'," said Raider.

"We're after the chief paymaster of the Southern Pacific," explained Doc.

"Doc . . ."

"Be sensible, Rade, we need all the help we can get."

Peace having been restored, people passed them coming and going. Doc took hold of Rodwell's arm, pulled him back into the alley, and told him about the assignment. And about Utterby's genius for disguising himself.

"We start to close in on him in one disguise and he switches to another."

"We don't know he's switched from her," said Raider, setting his jaw stubbornly.

"You haven't seen her around town today, have you? We couldn't walk half a block yesterday without seeing her. He's switched all right. To what, God only knows."

Rodwell rubbed his chin and considered the situation. "He can hang around here till next year."

Doc nodded.

"Or at least till he runs out of disguises. Sounds like you boys got your work cut out for you."

"Tell us somethin' we don't know," groused Raider.

The elderly man with the full white beard and the Congo cane passed by, his eyes straight ahead.

"Maybe he'll slip up," said Rodwell encouragingly.

"He hasn't yet. The only thing in our favor is, as you say, he'll probably hang around town while his stock goes up. If and when it levels off, he'll no doubt sell, then leave. Six times wealthier than when he arrived."

"He's got to have a room someplace, to sleep, change his disguises."

"He had a room at the American," said Doc, "but walked out and never came back."

"Did you check the other hotels?"

"What's the use? Whatever he's disguised as now is the only impression the desk clerk will have of him. Which can't do us any good."

"We could search every damn hotel room in town, Doc."

"There's six hotels," said Rodwell. "Upwards of a hundred and fifty rooms in all. Then too, you might not be able to get into some. They do everything they can to protect their guests."

"He's right, Rade. Deputy, the only angle we've been able to work so far is his horse. He left it with Arris Hunnicutt."

"If he's as clever as you say, when he does decide to leave he won't go back after it," said Rodwell. "In whatever disguise he's wearing at the time he'll just go and buy himself another horse. He'll sure be able to afford it."

Doc sighed. "Good Lord, that never occurred to me. It's just what he'll do."

"Cross your fingers he doesn't decide to leave."

"You boys know somethin'?" said Raider. "Lookin' for

a needle in a haystack is tough enough, but lookin' for him, not knowin' what he looks like, we don't know if he's a needle or a shoehorn or a sad iron or what. What I'm sayin' is we won't even know we've found him even if we do find him."

Rodwell stared. He looked hopelessly confused and somewhat fearful, as if worried that his mind had slipped a cog. "What did you say? What did he say?"

"I said—"

"Never mind, Rade, we get the picture."

"I got to be running," said Rodwell. "It's been nice chinnin' with you, and I do wish you luck."

"Better you wish us a damn miracle," said Raider.

"Right. And Raider, please don't get any sideline ideas about me. I've been on the straight and narrow for nearly five years, and I'm staying there."

"You're not our problem, Mason," said Doc. "All we want is Elmo Utterby. If you see anything, hear anything, we'd appreciate knowing. Good luck to you with the Claggetts."

Rodwell nodded and walked off. Raider and Doc started off in the opposite direction.

Doc took four steps and stopped short. "The picture."

Both turned around. Utterby's photograph hanging on the end of the hitch rack to dry was nowhere in sight.

"Son of a bitch," muttered Raider.

"Look around, it must have blown off."

They searched, unaware that it had not been blown off.

CHAPTER FIVE

WIRE RECEIVED ESHOLLENBECK RE NEW ANGLE
CASE ESTABLISHED BY YOU AND HIS HELP IN CON-
FIRMING SAME STOP HE STRESSES NEED FOR ALL
POSSIBLE DISPATCH IN APPREHENDING SUSPECT
AND RECOVERING MONEY STOP ALL THINGS CON-
SIDERED CASE APPEARS RUN OF MILL STOP SEE
NO REASON WHY YOU CANT BUTTON UP SAME
WITHIN FEW DAYS STOP DAILY PROGRESS RE-
PORTS WILL BE FORTHCOMING FROM YOU FROM
NOW ON STOP HOLLENBECK PRESSURING ME STOP
YOU UNDERSTAND STOP TRUST THAT BY TIME THIS
REACHES YOU YOU WILL HAVE CULPRIT IN CUS-
TODY STOP GOOD LUCK

There was no signature. No need for one. Raider snatched
the wire from Doc, crumpled it, and hurled it into a mound
of steaming horse manure in the middle of the street.

"'See no reason you can't button up same—'"

36

"Rade..."

"'—by time this reaches you.'"

"All right, all right."

"We don't have the son of a bitch's picture anymore, thanks to you leavin' it on the end o' that hitch rack in plain sight for anybody to lift."

"That was your idea!"

"All right, all right. He filched it, you know. We were busy jawin' with Rodwell, payin' no attention, he come by disguised as whatever, spotted it, and grabbed it, you betcha."

"An unusually vivid imagination."

"He did. Who else would?"

"Who says anybody did? It was blown away. Far away. There's no sense crying over spilt milk. It's no great loss, not with him moving from one disguise to another. Wait a minute, wait a minute."

"I'm not goin' anyplace."

They were sitting at a corner table in the Crystal Palace surrounded by babble, song, and gambling noise. Raider upended his tumbler, sending half a glass of Belcher's Whiskey, which to Doc tasted suspiciously like Valley Tan, down his throat.

"It's disgustin'," said Raider.

"Listen to me, Rade. Utterby visited Atherton as the lady in red. He purchased his stock, paid for it, and left with the certificates. What if he has to go back to the bank?"

"What for?"

"I don't know what for. Something. Anything. He can only go back as the lady, not as himself, not in any other disguise, isn't that so?"

"Go back for what?"

Doc waggled a finger and set his mind groping for an answer.

"What if... what if Atherton ordered a whole new issue printed. What if there was some flaw in the printing in the old certificates that might threaten their legality, and they had to be replaced. Everybody holding premium stock had to come to the bank to turn in their old certificates and get new ones in exchange."

"That's pretty thin, Doc."

"It's very thin. Give me a chance, I'll think of something. Some valid or at least seemingly valid excuse for Atherton to get him back to the bank."

"How can he do that when he doesn't know where to get in touch with him-her? He doesn't, you know, no more than we do."

"He wouldn't have to get in touch with him; all he would need to do is post a notice in the window: Public notice. In accordance with the laws of the Territory of Arizona all premium stockholders in the Big Bonanza Company are hereby invited—make that required—by law to attend a stockholders meeting for the purpose of determining the method by which dividends will be distributed. Date, time, etcetera, etcetera."

"You think Utterby'll get all tuckered out as the lady in red just to go to a damn meeting?"

"He'll have to, the law's the law."

"Bullshit. He'd be walkin' smack into a trap. He'll smell the rat; he won't go near the bank. He won't any more climb into his red dress than you or me. Besides, what makes you think Atherton'll play along? Not to mention all the other premium stockholders.

"You're startin' to get desperate, Doc. I know the signs, I've seen 'em before lotsa times. Don't go talkin' wild, desperate. Stay calm and think like Utterby. Long as he's hidin' behind a new disguise every day, every other day, he's safe as a baby in its mother's arms. But if he shows himself without a disguise or wears a disguise, changes it for another, then goes back and uses the first one a second time, he's askin' for big trouble. He's takin' a chance he doesn't have to take. If I can figure that out, don't you think he can too?"

"I guess."

"I know. He's got his stock bought and paid for. There's nothin' the law or the bank or anybody can do to take it away from him. Is there? Course not. He knows that; he knows he'll never have to go near the bank again, and he won't risk losin' out in any way. You can't take somethin' away from somebody just because they don't jump through your hoop when you ask 'em to."

"All right, all right."

"Your trouble is you're thinkin' like you think he thinks, not like *he* thinks."

"Shut up, Rade!"

"What are you gettin' sore about?"

"You've made your point. You don't have to beat it to death. Instead of knocking down my ideas, how about coming up with some of your own?"

Raider poured and drank, wiped his mouth with his sleeve, and grinned the grin of a man who's just been called and *knows* he's holding the winning hand.

"I thought you'd never ask me."

His mouth was open, but before he could get another word out a woman spoke.

"Hi, fellas, are you lonesome? I'm thirsty. I'm Eloisa. Not Eloise, Eloisa with an 'a' on the end."

"Go jump in a well," snarled Raider.

"Rade..."

"Can'cha see you're interruptin' a serious conversation?"

"You're rude!"

"You are, Rade. Eloisa, he doesn't know any bet—"

It was as far as Doc got. His first three words had been uttered while he impaled Raider with his iciest glare. By the time he got to the lady's name he had turned to look at her. Four and a half words later he recognized her dress.

"Where did you get that dress?"

"Huh?"

"Your dress, where did you get it?"

"What's the matter with you, mister? He's rude. What are you, crackers?"

"Please, just tell me where you got the dress!"

"You like it? I bought it from a fella, an ol' man with a white beard. Carried a cane, walked kinda bent over. I swear I don't know what he was doin' with this dress, but he showed it to me and a hat with ostrich feathers and a matchin' parasol, and I just never seen nothin' so bee-yootiful in all my born days. I paid him five bucks cash."

"Describe him," rasped Doc.

"I just did."

"Yes, yes, thank you, thank you. Come on, Rade."

"I haven't finished my drinkin'."

"Yes, you have!"

By the time he got Raider outside Doc was so excited he was having trouble getting his breath. "We've got to find him, white beard, cane, before he changes disguises!"

"Oh horseshit. We could run aroun' like two hens with our heads lopped off turnin' over every rock, every barrel, and never find him. He's changed getups again."

"You don't know that."

"Like I keep sayin', you're not thinkin' like he's thinkin'. I am, and I'm thinkin' here's a floozy just about my dress size. I'll peddle her my red dress with all the trimmins', those two Pinkerton assholes are bound to see her and recognize it, they'll ask her where she got it, she'll say old man with a white beard and by the time they get aroun' to lookin' for me I'll be a Baptist preacher with a paintbrush beard, the Good Book, hard collar and all, or a tinhorn gambler with a wax mustache with the points sharp as darts and a pointy beard."

"All right, all right."

"He's playin' games with us, Doc. Don't play with him. Don't give him the satisfaction. I'm not."

"Before we were interrupted you were about to tell me your bright idea. I'm all ears."

"It's about time. This is it: as of now, I mean right this second, we stop lookin' for Utterby."

"Rade..."

Raider stopped him with his upraised hand. "Far as we're concerned he's disappeared. Insteada him we look for his stuff, his costumes, his makeup kit, his stock certificates. He's got to be stayin' somewhere, and they got to be with him. He wouldn't leave the certificates with fatso Mr. Candy at the bank. He took 'em with him; he's keepin' 'em with him."

"You're talking about going through all the rooms in all the hotels in town, Rade."

Again up came his hand. "Not us. We don't lift a finger. Let me ask you somethin'. Who's the one person gets to go into every room in every hotel? Not the manager, not the desk clerk; like Rodwell says, guests can kick up quite a fuss when you ask to search their rooms."

"To answer your question, the chambermaid."

"Right! You're smart, Weatherbee, you really are. You catch on quick."

"Shut up."

"Don't be rude. Ha! Be honest. Is that a good idea or is that a great idea?"

"Let's say it's the only one we've got at the moment. Why don't you get started on it? You might just as well begin at the American Hotel. I'll join you later."

"Where you goin'?"

"You saw the chief's telegram. He wants a progress report. If we don't send him something he'll have his son Bill or Robert, somebody chasing out here. I'll cook up something. At least keep them at bay another twenty-four hours. I'll see you in about half an hour, and be careful, Rade, don't tell the chambermaids any more than you have to. Just say you're looking for a guest with a makeup case. No need to mention the certificates. They'll likely be hidden anyway."

"And his costumes."

"I suppose you can ask about them, too. Offer them twenty-five dollars if they can find him. On one condition:

that they keep it secret. I'll see you later."

> CLOSING IN ON EU STOP SPORADIC HOSTILITIES
> IN AREA MAY DELAY ACTUAL CAPTURE BUT SAME
> INEVITABLE STOP BULK STOLEN MONEY IN-
> VESTED MINING STOCK WHICH HAPPILY FORE-
> STALLS INDISCRIMINATE SQUANDERING STOP WILL
> KEEP YOU INFORMED DAILY AS PER REQUEST
>
> W

Doc emerged from the Western Union office feeling considerably more optimistic about things in general than an hour earlier. Raider was right, as usual—the makeup case was the key to finding Utterby. He might possibly be carrying the certificates on him, but it was doubtful he'd be carrying the makeup case. The clothing for his various disguises he could purchase right here in town, and dispose of the outfits as soon as they outlived their usefulness, as he already had with Eloisa.

Raider. For a boy from a hog farm in northeastern Arkansas who had left school forever at the ripe old age of ten, who had probably not read so much as a single book all the way through in his entire life, whose handwriting resembled a six-year-old's and vocabulary made liberal use of grunts, unintelligible mutterings, and other noises, the man was brilliant. He had an innate shrewdness that neatly blended with his trail smarts. He had as well a unique capacity for putting himself not only in the culprit's boots, but virtually inside his or her head. Witness the situation at hand. He was absolutely right when he said Utterby would never return to the bank under any circumstances. Doing so would be tantamount to returning to the scene of his crime.

"He's brilliant."

"Ond who might thot be, Weatherbee?"

CHAPTER SIX

The cold fist of fear seized Doc's heart and squeezed it so he nearly yelled aloud. He slowly turned. Into view came the last person in the Western world he would have wished to look upon. Allan Pinkerton, his face deeply etched with the exhaustion and illness he had been afflicted with for the past three years, his salt-and-pepper beard thrust forward like the cowcatcher on a locomotive, his eyes riveting in defiance of the ear-to-ear smile that stretched his face, waved a large, misshapen finger.

"Cot got your tongue?"

"Chief..."

Up marched Allan Pinkerton, his smile still plastered in place, his breath exhaling sibilantly from his nostrils.

"Sooprise, sooprise. Exploonations are in order tae be shoor. I was doon south in Phoenix, a virulent rathool oov a place, ooverrun with mooney-grobbing parasites, fierce sovages, ond Mexicans oon the run from the law, ond Will Wogner onformed me by wire thot E. S. Hoolenbock was

43

becooming ooverly distoorbed by this oombezzlement business, choomping ot the proverbial bit. Being so close, I decided tae stop oop ond tooch bases with you two before heading for Chicago. Speaking oov two, where is the cowboy with the nosty tongue, the weak stoomoch, ond the penchant for doxies? Flown the coop, hos he?"

"No, sir, he's working on an angle. I'm just on my way to join him."

Pinkerton slipped an arm through Doc's. "Wot are we waiting for? Oon the way you con fill me in oon the case. Hov you caught Ootterby yet? Are you about to? Is the trop aboot tae be sprooong? Speak, lod, I'm all ears."

His heart thudding like a smith's hammer, Doc stumbled through an explanation of the case and their sadly limited success in solving it thus far. Walking side by side with Pinkerton, he did not have to turn to see the chief's homely face darken by degrees. He could actually *feel* his mounting disappointment as his pink-lobed ears absorbed his words.

They reached the front of the American Hotel.

"In short, stripped oov the beating about the boosh, the oxcuses, the rotionalizations and ootright cloptrop, whot you're saying is you're noo better oof thon whon you coom tae toon."

"Not at all. We know he bought the stock; we know he's sticking around to keep tabs on the mine's productivity and its effect on his investment; we know he's changing from one disguise to another."

"In soom you hoven't the vaguest idea where tae lay honds oon the snake. It would oppear I've orrived in the nick oov time."

She was Mexican, with dark, luminous eyes, a flawless copper-toned complexion, and a smile calculated to melt a man's heart. She boasted a most impressive team of breasts and a figure to complement them that in a tight-fitting gown would have brought a lump to Raider's throat. However, she was wearing the frumpy, nondescript uniform of a chambermaid, and her sleek black hair, which he envisioned tumbling down to and below her shoulders, was pulled back and bound in a tight knot.

She sat on the end of the bed. He stood with his back to the door, arms folded, hands tucked under his armpits, as if to keep them from attacking.

"There's ten bucks in it for you, señorita. All you got to do is track down that makeup kit."

"Why does he have such a thing, is he an actor?"

"Yeah. Bad actor."

"You don't want to tell me what's going on." She smiled and shrugged. "What do I care?"

She rose from the end of the bed, bringing his eyes upward with her breasts. He swallowed. She smiled a different smile.

"Come here," she commanded.

He almost stumbled walking over to her. She began to unbutton her shirt.

She bucked, taking his cock up to the root, nearly fracturing his pelvis in her eagerness to engorge him. Her massive breasts slapped loudly against his naked chest, and she squealed and sank her teeth into his shoulder.

Bucked, bucked, bucked. Fucked, fucked, fucked. She was a fucking machine. The frightening impression crossed his mind that had there been a hundred of him and only one of her, she would have bucked as wildly, shrilled as excitedly, abused and drained as completely the last one as she did this. He had fucked women from border to border in every state and territory west of the Big Muddy. He had screwed stone, he had screwed fire, and every conceivable type between, but never before had he saddled a machine. By comparison she made an unbroken mustang seem docile. She was neither flesh nor bone, but Pittsburgh steel. She adored cock and couldn't get enough of his. He dimly wondered if she was trying to snap it free, take it inside her, seal her lips, cross her legs, and he'd never see it again. If any woman could commit such a horrible crime it was this one.

Not coming, not enjoyment, but surviving intact was uppermost in his mind.

"Easy, easy, for Chrissakes, you'll break it off."

She growled, shrilled, bit, hung on, and pumped even more vigorously. A knock sounded at the door. He froze; she ignored it, continuing her merciless assault, upthrusting, gyrating.

"What the hell . . ." he began.

A second knock.

"Rade, are you there? Rade, I can hear you."

"Go away. Come back later."

Still she fucked, with not so much as a hint of acknowledgment of the interruption showing in her eyes.

"Rade . . ."

"Beat it!"

"*Raider!*"

His eyes started from his head, his jaw dropped, he gaped. On she drove, throwing her head from side to side, her moist and swollen tongue hanging from her mouth lasciviously, her insatiable lust finding voice in husky, animal-like intonations.

That voice! Pinkerton! It couldn't be! Impossible."

He jerked upright, whipped his cock free.

"What are you doing? *Caramba! Loco gringo!* Back in, stick it back in! In!"

She grabbed his cock, pulling it cuntward.

"Owwwwww! What the hell you doin'!"

"Rade . . ."

"Raider, oopen this door at once, mon!"

Two fists rapped loudly. Raider seized her wrist and squeezed it.

"Ow!"

She released his cock and let loose a torrent of curses. He jumped from the bed.

"Up, up," he hissed. "Into the closet."

"You go to hell."

Again the knocking.

"I'm coming, I'm coming. Cover up, cover up. I gotta let 'em in. Got to!"

"You do and I will scratch your eyes out, *gringo* bastard! I will rip your face from your head!"

"Raider!"

"Rade..."

He grabbed the sheet beneath her and jerked it forth in the manner of a magician pulling a tablecloth from under a table setting complete with a glass filled with wine. He flung the sheet over her, went to the door, was about to open it, realized that he himself was scarcely presentable, returned to the bed, retrieved his pants, and pulled them on. Buckling his belt with one hand, he unlocked the door with the other. It flew inward, smashing him in the nose.

"Owwwww! Goddamn it!"

In strode Allan Pinkerton, Doc following, hurling his eyes heavenward at his partner.

"You busted my nose!"

"Serves you right. Stond bock when you oopen a door, you jockoss, and you'll nae cotch it in the noose. Ah hah, joost os I thought!"

"She's sick abed, can'cha see? I was walkin' down the hall and the door was a little open, you know, and she asked me to come in to give her some medical advice."

"Oh shut oop, you oncorrigible nincompoop! Dinna make yourself look ony more holf-witted thon you do olready. Get your shirt oon ond coom doonstairs with Weatherbee ond me. We've a case in our lops, we've no time for your filthy oxtracurriculor octivities."

"I gotta go," Raider said to the girl.

"Go to hell for all I care!" This was followed by a second torrent of curses and insults in Spanish.

Stepping into his boots, putting on his shirt and tucking it in, Raider went out into the hallway and closed the door behind him, muffling but not entirely silencing her continuing diatribe.

"I can explain real easy, chief."

"I'm nae onterested. It dinna sooprise me. You've the morals oov on alley cat in heat. You should be mortally oshamed oov yourself, boot oov course you never hove been. March, ond two steps behind if you dinna mind. Hoopfully those we poss will nae ossociate you with the two oov os."

Chief Pinkerton refused to hold the council of war in a restaurant for fear they would be charged for water and toothpicks. He refused to repair to a watering hole because he did not drink and "would nae troost the soft bevoroges or cow's milk ovailable in sooch disrooputoble places."

They settled for the lobby of the Macomber Lodging House. It resembled a thousand other lobbies, smelled like them, and the overstuffed chairs were occupied by the usual coterie of loungers: newspaper readers, smokers, starers into space, sleepers.

"I'll pretend thot the disgoosting spectacle I joost witnessed hos nae taken place, ond we'll start from scrotch. You're fortunate I'm forgiving by nature, ond thot the press oov business dictates we move forward instead oov sideways."

"Thanks, chief."

"Dinna thonk me, you ninnyhommer, thonk your looky stars. Whon Weatherbee here told me oov your plon to ongage the coonfidence oov the various chombermaids aboot toon it strook me thot the idea hod merit. Hooever, oofering thom a reword for trocking doon Ootterby's makeoop case is one thing, climbing into bed with thom quite anoother. Hod you it in mind to ossault every one in toon os part oov your deal?"

"No, sir, I didn't assault her, she did me. She undressed me, she—"

"Please, spare oos the porticulors."

Allan Pinkerton may have been a towering prude and monumentally disdainful of Operative Raider's sexual shenanigans, but this did not blind him to the value of his plan.

Indeed, he saw fit to compliment him on putting himself in Utterby's shoes, thinking like him, and concentrating on the makeup case instead of the man in their search. Nevertheless, as Doc sat listening to him elaborate on the idea, inundate them with unsolicited advice on how to carry it out, and proffer his assistance, his heart couldn't help but sag in his chest. However good his intentions, the chief would only hamstring them.

Still, he was a remarkable man. In 1842, at the age of twenty-three, he had emigrated from Glasgow, Scotland, to Chicago. A year later he moved to Dundee, Illinois, where he established a cooperage business. Here he ran down a gang of conterfeiters and as a result was appointed deputy sheriff of Kane County and immediately afterwards of Cook County, with headquarters in Chicago. It was there that he organized a force of detectives, which he preferred to call operatives, to capture thieves who stole large sums of money from express companies. In 1866 his agency captured the principals in the theft of $700,000 from Adams Express Company safes on a train of the New York, New Haven & Hartford railway, and recovered all but about $12,000 of the stolen money.

In February 1861 he found evidence of a plot to assassinate President-elect Lincoln upon his arrival in Baltimore on his way to Washington; as a result, Lincoln passed through Baltimore at an early hour in the morning without stopping. In April 1861, Pinkerton, on the suggestion of General George B. McClellan, organized a system of obtaining military information in the Southern states. From this system he developed the Federal Secret Service, of which he was in charge throughout the war, under the assumed name of Major E. J. Allen.

In 1869 he suffered a partial stroke of paralysis, and thereafter the management of the detective agency devolved chiefly on his sons, William and Robert.

He was one of a kind and, despite his "semi-retirement," continued to dabble in investments when and where he found

it convenient. Convenience had no part in his dabbling in
the private lives of his operatives; it was a lifelong habit
that most of the targets of his nosiness either took good-
naturedly or ignored altogether. He did not dabble in Doc's
private life; he could not resist dabbling in Raider's. Doc
repeatedly assured his partner that Pinkerton's prying was
purely out of a fatherly affection for him. If the chief didn't
have a warm place in his heart for him he wouldn't have
bothered. Raider disagreed. To him the chief was a med-
dlesome old lady. On more than one occasion the two had
engaged in heated discussions. More than once Raider had
threatened to quit. Twice he actually did, only to eventually
succumb to his partner's pleas (or pretend to succumb) and
change his mind.

Deep in his heart Raider harbored grudging admiration
for the old man. As a young man, Allan Pinkerton was a
typically taciturn Scot, muscular, intense, ready to fight with
his fists in defense of his rights or of those he sided with.
His abolitionist activities embroiled him in many a contro-
versy. Stubborn, quick-tempered, and aggressive, he would
not hesitate to wade into a fight against odds that would
frighten a less impulsive man.

In establishing his detective agency, he was determined
that the public look upon his firm as a profession rather than
a business. He called himself the "principal" and his in-
vestigators "operatives." A client was expected to produce
credentials, identification, and reasonable need for services
for Pinkerton to sit down for an interview. If the case was
accepted, a "journal" was prepared. In it would be the record
of the case, the problems, requirements, and the detailed
plan of operation which the operatives in the field would
be required to follow.

The agency operated under a strict code of ethics. Pinkerton's *General Principles* became the guide rules for the
agency. The agency would not represent a defendant in a
criminal case except with the knowledge and consent of the
prosecutor; operatives would not shadow jurors or investi-

gate public officials in the performance of their duties, or trade-union officers or members in their lawful union activities; they would not accept employment from one political party against another; they would not work for vice crusaders; they would not accept contingent fees, gratuities, or rewards. The agency would never investigate the morals of a woman unless in connection with another crime, nor would it handle cases of divorce or other scandalous matters.

One iron-spined philosophy ran through the *General Principles:* that the end justifies the means, if the end was the accomplishment of justice.

The chief's personal drive and ambition were awesome, and neither seemed to slacken with age. He ruled his home as he did the agency—with an iron hand of a tyrant. He had his own way of doing things, which was the only way. He was intransigent, vindictive, fiercely opinionated, resentful of criticism, and absolutely fearless, brilliant in his chosen profession, incorruptible, devoted to family, friends, and employees, and deeply respected by the public at large.

Little wonder deep down Raider respected, perhaps even liked the man. He had been embarrassed and penitent when the chief caught him "in the act" and immediately after when he heaped coals upon his head. Now that the storm was past, however, and the conversation dealt solely with the case, Raider's attitude was changing. Doc recognized the signs. Irritation was displacing his shame. The longer Pinkerton droned on, the more upset he appeared to become. He didn't want the old man meddling, didn't want him in town, in the territory. And he was on the verge of telling him so in very certain terms.

As Pinkerton prattled on, dominating the conversation, Doc held his breath. On top of everything else, all they needed was another blowup between the Scot and the plowboy.

In a room on the floor above the Pinkertons, directly over their heads, Elmo Utterby wrapped up the old man's jacket, trousers, and cane in an old newspaper and laid the package on the end of the bed. He restored the white beard and eyebrows to his makeup case. He cast a glance at his photo, which he had spotted and plucked from the end of the hitch rack earlier and which now occupied a corner of the mirror.

"Not very flattering, old boy."

He chuckled, then sobered. Pride set his chest glowing warmly. He had pulled it off, precisely as he'd planned it. After twenty-two years of slaving over the company's books under the relentless, red-rimmed eye of Jabez Frome, who spent two-thirds of his adult life in a state of semi-intoxication, who babbled rather than talked, found fault with everything and everyone in the office, browbeat the small fry, and toadied to the bigwigs, in short was a thoroughly reprehensible excuse for a human being, he, Elmo Utterby, had taken his place. Someone had to; Jabez had fallen down drunk as a lord in the street and been run over by a wagon loaded with whiskey barrels. A more appropriate demise could not have been planned.

So after twenty-two years the tree of Elmo's patience finally bore the fruit he had so long prayed for. Summoned to the office of Everett Scott Hollenbeck, he had been awarded Frome's job. Henceforth, Hollenbeck informed him, Elmo Utterby would be the chief paymaster of the Southern Pacific. That night he had gone out and gotten gloriously drunk. He had awakened the next morning with a blacksmith shop inside his head. He was suffering mightily, but he was happier than he had ever been in his life.

It wasn't until about a week later that his joy over his good fortune began to abate. By the end of the first month it had all but vanished. The job brought with it a $2,200 per annum increase in salary. Responsibility for paying everyone from the office sweeper up to the president and board of directors their correct pay to the penny rested solely on his shoulders. A responsibility it was, and he welcomed it; it offered the ultimate challenge to his talents, his intelligence, and his love of exactitude. He did his job perfectly. The paymaster's office had never run more smoothly; morale had never been higher; compliments from the higher-ups fell on everyone's ears almost daily.

He should have been sitting on top of the world, and except for one thing he would have been. Every week in between paydays a memo would arrive at his desk from Hollenbeck or one of the vice-presidents, requesting that a check be made out to cash and dispatched to the requester. The amounts were often considerable, up to five, even ten thousand dollars. What possible "expenses" could be so costly he had no idea. He kept a record of each officer's amounts and at the end of his first six months on the job discovered that Hollenbeck alone had siphoned nearly $70,000 out of the business and into his pockets.

Everyone at the top, without exception, was stealing from the company, and it was his job to help them by concealing their thievery. From Hollenbeck on down every officer was well paid, if not overpaid. The Southern Pacific was doing well, freight tonnage and rates rose steadily year after year; passenger miles too were up. The straw that broke the camel's back was placed about fourteen months after Elmo had taken over for the unfortunate Frome. His assistant, Wilfred Trimble, had just become the father of twins; the man came to him, explained his financial situation, and asked for a raise of $2 a week. Utterby was perfectly willing to grant the raise, but in his readiness to do so, he yielded to the temptation to phrase his agreement in the form of a promise.

He went immediately to Vice-President J. B. Cantor's office and explained the situation and Trimble's pressing need for the increase. Cantor heard him out politely, then turned him down, citing a small, almost trivial monthly dip in revenues, which both knew was seasonal, as a possible sign of a long-term downward trend.

He asked Cantor's permission to speak to Hollenbeck. Permission was granted. To his amazement, Hollenbeck also refused the request; his excuse: "J. B. turned it down; his judgment's worth its weight in gold to me."

He went back to his own office, called in his assistant, and told him the bad news. Trimble was stunned; he thanked Utterby for trying and went back to work. Ten minutes later a memo arrived from J. B. Cantor requesting $4,500 immediately for expenses incurred on a business trip to San Mateo, a stone's throw south of San Francisco. He made out the check to cash, entered it in the books as expenses, called in an office boy, and handed him the envelope to be delivered to Cantor's office.

He spent the next two weeks evolving his plan. Before pilfering a penny for himself he brazenly wrote out a check to cash for expenses to E. S. Hollenbeck in the amount of $1,000, cashed it in the strongbox in the office safe, and that night under the cover of darkness slipped the money through his assistant's open bedroom window while the man, his wife, and their twins slept.

"The rest is history, old boy."

Artfully disguised as the lady in red, he had departed the American Hotel without formally checking out, which would have betrayed his identity. Merely walking out as the lady, he could register elsewhere as her. He signed into the Saguaro House. The next day he performed the same ritual, exiting the Saguaro House as the white-bearded old man with the Congo cane.

This disguise, too, had outlived its usefulness; now he would assume the guise of a doctor, complete with bag and layman's basic knowledge of the art. It was the most fun he had had in years, in perhaps his whole life. The acting company back home was loads of fun, but one wasn't always at liberty to choose one's role. In this performance he could assume whatever role he pleased. Moreover, it was a solo act, a one-man show; the stage, the spotlight, the audience—his pursuers—were his and his alone.

Loads of fun, and most hilarious of all was the attraction to "her" of the one called Raider.

"He couldn't take his eyes off you! A pity he'll never see you again."

He had wrapped the stock certificates carefully and placed them in a shoe box on the closet shelf. His makeup case was kept out of sight under whatever bed he happened to be sleeping in that night, away from the prying eyes and prattling tongue of the chambermaid. The thought of the chambermaid made him stop and think. Perhaps with all the precautions he was taking, he still wasn't being as careful as he might be.

"Should be, old boy."

If his pursuers got it into their heads to bribe every chambermaid in town to look for his makeup case it could wind up in catastrophe. There must be fifteen or twenty chambermaids all told in the six hotels in town; that the people chasing him might approach them all seemed improbable, but not impossible. If they approached one they'd have to approach them all.

He had set the makeup case on the bed. He glanced about the room. Where could he hide it? It measured approximately 16 inches long by 10 inches wide, and 6 high. Not something he could slip under the mattress. He went to the window, raised it, and leaned out. The view was blocked by the brick wall of the building next door; it was so close he could almost reach out and touch it. The narrow alley below was impassable, blocked with broken barrels and trash of one sort or another. It looked as if the roomers on that side of the hotel used it for a trash pit.

The ledge outside the window extended six inches past the frame on either side. He might set the case on end and leave it there temporarily. No one passed below, and it would scarcely be noticed from the street. The idea was good but begged refinement. Why not buy some cord, tie one end around the case, and lower it into the trash below? The cord would never be noticed from the street, and the free end could be wedged under the extended ledge out of sight of anyone looking through the window.

"Elmo, old boy, your genius never ceases to amaze me."

The first order of business upon leaving the Macomber would be to purchase a ball of twine. An hour later he tucked the wrapped-up old man's outfit and cane under his arm and left. He descended the stairs to the lobby disguised as a middle-aged doctor wearing a fedora, thick-rimmed, clear-glass spectacles, a flowing mustache and Van Dyke beard. He wore a slate gray linen suit, doeskin gloves, and carried a medical bag complete with stethoscope, a prop he had acquired while playing the role of the doctor in *Hearts of the West,* which ran for nineteen weeks and was cited by the drama critic of the San Francisco *Examiner* as "utterly charming."

He passed three men deep in conversation in the lobby. He recognized "Rade" and his partner; Doc was it? The cowboy looked straight at him. Then he got up and confronted him. His heart skipped a beat, then another. Did he recognize him? Had he penetrated his disguise? How could he!

"Doc . . ."

"Yes?"

"Would you mind lookin' at my nose?"

"Rade . . ." began Doc.

Allan Pinkerton stared, mystified.

"I think it's busted. Feels like it."

"Let's have a look."

In the twinkling of an eye he was once again Dr. Bassett in *Hearts of the West.*

"It's *been* broken."

"Four times, this is the fifth."

"Are both nostrils open? Can you breathe properly?"

"Yeah, but it still hurts like hell."

"Afraid you'll have to settle for four."

"You sure?"

"Listen to your doctor."

Raider seemed genuinely disappointed. He mumbled thanks.

The doctor touched his hat and resumed his approach to the doors. He stopped two steps from them, turned, and retraced his path. Ascending the stairs, he went into his room, removed his picture from the corner of the mirror, wet it in the washbasin, crumpled it, and tossed it out the window.

"You really should be more careful, old boy. It's always the little things that trip one up. 'Is my nose busted?' Ha ha, priceless. Beautiful! I love it!"

Raider followed the doctor out the lobby doors with his eyes. Moments later a perspiring Marshal Rhilander and Mason Rodwell came in. As the day wore on it was getting hotter out, threatening the onset of a savage heat wave. Their appearance brought a frown to Raider's face.

"What now?" Doc asked him.

"Rodwell hadda go and tell his nibs who we are, why we come here."

"Why shouldn't he?"

"Awwww..."

Doc introduced Allan Pinkerton to Rhilander and the deputy.

"I heard you'd arrived in town, sir," said the marshal. "Deputy Rodwell here and I've been out looking for all three of you. I'll get right to the point."

"Thot would be oppreciated, Marshal."

"We know you've got your hands full with a case here—"

"Oh, do you noo?" The chief's steely gaze drifted to Raider, then Doc.

"We've got a problem too."

He expounded at length on the Claggetts, their hit-and-run tactics, and the demoralizing effect they were having on the town in general and his staff in particular.

"They just don't quit. No wonder some of our most reliable boys are getting discouraged. We've got the youngest, Elon, locked up, and he'll be going up for trial late next week. A flock of witnesses saw the shoot-out in the Crystal Palace the other day. Your two men here did. The jury won't have any trouble finding him guilty."

"Hoopfully for your sake."

"The thing of it is, sir, before, during, or maybe even after the trial his brothers are sure to show up and try to spring him. They've already tried once. When they come back next time they'll be overloaded for bear. They've got friends out there, they could come in force. Innocent people may be killed. The short of it is it's certain bloodshed I'd like to prevent. The only way we can do that is beat them out of the chute. Mount a posse, go out to their place, surround it, and take them. Maybe even wipe them out. The thing of it is—"

"The thing oov it is you'll need oll the guns you con get, eh, lod?"

"Yes, sir. As I said before, some of the boys are getting discouraged. You could even say disgusted. Ready to wash their hands of the whole mess. The deputy and I were hoping you might see your way clear to lend us your two operatives. Their joining up might even encourage others to throw in."

"I see. Oonfortunately, mooch os I opplaud your thinking ond your coorage, I'm ofraid we'll hov to decline."

"But—"

"We're oonder a great deal oov pressure to close this one oot with the ootmost dispotch. We can nae allow oorselves tae be sidetrocked by your doomestic squabbles."

Rhilander's face darkened perceptibly. "Is that your final word?"

"It is. I'm soory."

The marshal shrugged, jerked his head at Rodwell, and they left.

Exasperation tightened the chief's features. "Raider, tell me hoo he ond his deputy knew aboot you ond your 'problem.'"

"He didn't tell Rodwell," said Doc. "I did. Rade was annoyed, he didn't want to, I thought we should. At the time I thought if we could help them we could get a *quid pro quo* out of it."

"Ot the time thot was good thinking, lod."

Raider bristled. "What the hell you tell him that for?"

"Wot's your trooble?"

"When you thought *I* told 'em you wanted to chew my ears off; when you found out *he* did you pat him on the damn back!"

"Foosh, dinna go firin' your face ot me, mon, ond dinna be daft. I had nae intention oov chewing your ears off. I've better things tae mosticate. Speaking oov which, isn't it getting close tae sooper time? Let's eat while we discoos this chombermaid idea. By the way, Weathorbee, wot's hoppened tae your Boston derby hot?"

"It took a bullet through it."

"Good losh, I hoop your head was nae inside it ot the time."

Raider made a gravelly sound deep in his throat, which Doc took to signify an accusation of stark stupidity on the part of the chief. Then Raider threw up his hands and marched off.

CHAPTER SEVEN

They stood outside the restaurant, attacking their teeth with toothpicks, Raider's and Doc's wooden, Pinkerton's gold, the gift of his wife Joan. The sky, which had been the pale pink of a shorthorn steer's muzzle when they went in to eat, had deepened to a vivid crimson, and the setting sun sizzled and shimmered like an egg yolk.

"Each oov oos will take two hoostelries," said the chief, "ond approach the chombermaids os Weathorbee soggests. Osk them tae look oot for the coolprit's makeoop case."

"As I suggested," corrected Raider.

"That's right," said Doc. "He did."

"'Tis nae impoortont who. If you foncy a goold star for your every idea, Raider, I'm soory tae disoppoint you. Noo then—"

A shot rang, followed by a flurry, then a fusillade. A host of riders came sweeping into town.

"Oh my God," murmured Doc.

"Wot . . ." began the chief.

"Hit the dirt!" boomed Raider. He did so instantly, though not so fast he bumped his tender nose. And not before he recognized two of the Claggetts leading the invaders.

The gang carried torches. As one they turned up the main street and headed for the marshal's office at the far end. Reaching it in seconds, they flung their fire onto the roof. By now the entire street was alive with indignation, fear, and hysteria. Men, women, even older boys began firing at the outlaws. Marshal Rhilander, Mason Rodwell, and four other deputies came boiling out of the office slinging lead. A brief skirmish took place on the spot, driving two of the deputies back inside and spreading the others and the marshal to the sides seeking cover. The outlaws too began to take cover. Within sixty seconds the entire street became a battleground. Raider, Doc, and the chief had by now withdrawn to the locked front door of the restaurant. Patrons and employees inside crowded the window to watch the gunplay until a stray shot shattered it, sending everyone fleeing further inside, screaming and bellowing in retreat. The chief pounded on the door, demanding it be opened. Raider calmly stepped inside through the broken window. Doc followed, as did Pinkerton.

Up on the roof of the marshal's office two men appeared and began to beat out the flames with blankets.

"Their kid brother's in there," rasped Raider, "and the stupid idiots try to burn the place down."

Residents and deputies alike kept up a steady fire at the invaders. It became difficult to differentiate the outlaws from the defenders. Two members of the gang appeared on roofs and began to unload. A rifle shot caught one in the brisket as soon as he showed, tumbling him face forward into the street, cracking his neck sickeningly.

The firing continued. A pall of smoke began to gather over the street. It hung like morning mist over a swamp. People on both sides had been wounded, and at least six killed outright. Marshal Rhilander and his men continued to defend the office, keeping the attackers clear of it, preventing any further damage, and blocking any attempt to get to Elon, who was locked in a cell inside.

It was a typical Claggett foray, decided Doc—all noise and activity, the air filled with lead, but with no recognizable strategy. Raider spotted a man twisting around the corner of the Merchandise Mart diagonally opposite, preparing to gun down the American Hotel clerk, whose head was down, his attention on reloading. Raider took careful aim and blew the would-be killer away with one shot, sending him flying over backwards. A man hitherto unseen behind him took his place and returned fire. Raider roared and fell on his side, hit in the leg just above the knee. Doc and the chief pulled him back from the broken window. Luckily, his assailant did not follow up; another man took his attention and his fire.

Meanwhile, some of the Claggetts and their followers had mounted up and were barreling away, loosing a withering fire to both sides to clear a path. Two of them, from their faces brothers or cousins, pulled up right in front of where Doc and the chief were ministering to Raider. One aimed his rifle straight at Pinkerton.

"You, old man, you're comin' with us!"

"Stoof ond noonsense."

He fired. The shot passeed squarely between the chief's legs, striking the floor behind him.

"Come outta there!"

The other man covered Doc.

"Take me," Doc rasped. "Not him." He rose slowly, raising his hands, dropping his .38 Diamondback.

The one who fired laughed. "He's the one we want, dude, not you."

In a twinkling their hostage was up behind the shooter, and off they thundered. Doc retrieved his gun, braced it on his free forearm, and took careful aim.

"Don't try, Doc, you'll hit him."

Slowly Doc lowered the gun. "My God."

* * *

Two minutes later the last shot was fired, the last outlaws were gone, leaving in their wake two wounded and four dead of their own. Raider's wound was painful but not serious. The patrons and employees gathered around them. Passerbys stopped and gaped. Along came the doctor who had examined Raider's nose earlier. He took one look and ordered him to pull down his trousers. Raider demurred, the onlookers laughed, the doctor insisted it was the only way he could properly examine him. Doc insisted, the onlookers insisted, Raider gave in. He folded his trousers neatly and laid them across his crotch.

The doctor checked out his wound. "You're a lucky man," he said, straightening up.

"Tell me about it."

"I mean it, it must have been a ricochet. It's no more than an inch in. I'll have it out in a jiffy."

"You mean here and now in front o' this buncha gawkers?"

"I don't mind working with an audience. Would you prefer being hauled over to my office? It's up to you: a little pain here, or a lot moving you there and a little more on top of it."

"Get it out and over with," said Doc. "We've got things to do."

"You do, maybe, but not this boy. He's going from here straight to bed."

"Oh for Chrissakes, whatta you talkin' about? It's just a damn flesh wound. You get it out, I'll get up and do a little dance for you."

"Just be quiet and hold still. Would you folks please back off and give the patient a little air? You—Doc, is it? Get a shot of something from the bartender."

Raider downed a shot glass of whiskey in one gulp, asked for another, and was turned down. The doctor thrust a tongue depresser in his mouth and ordered him to bite hard. Raider snapped it in two.

"Not that hard, for pity's sakes."

"You didn't say how hard."

The doctor gave him another. Then he washed the wound with a dash of carbolic acid straight from the bottle. Raider's face purpled, his eyes bulged, his bite held, and sweat poured from him. The crowd oohed and ahhed, everyone feeling the pain. The doctor dug, explored, located the slug, and eased it forth to a round of applause. He stanched the bleeding, applied a gauze pad, and bandaged the leg.

"One of you boys give this man a hand. Get hold of a plank," he said to Doc. "Get him into bed. See that you stay there, Wild Bill. Stay off that leg for at least a week. Check and see if it's still bleeding about this time tomorrow. It should start knitting in earnest in about forty-eight hours. Keep your hands off it." He turned to Doc and handed him a roll of gauze. "Change the dressing in twenty-four hours, then every other day."

Doc gave him three dollars for his services, and off he went, followed by the onlookers' applause. The show was over. The crowd broke up.

"What the hell do we do now?" asked Raider when they were once more by themselves. "What in red hell did they go and take him for? Why him?"

"Who knows, Rade? It could be they recognized him. Oh Lord, what made me say that?"

CHAPTER EIGHT

Virgil Claggett belched, ran a greasy sleeve under his runny nose, and set his bulk on a three-legged stool in the middle of the floor of the dingy, filthy, depressing room. To Allan Pinkerton, when approaching the house with his captors, the place looked as if it had blown down, been reduced to kindling, and then rebuilt from the pieces. By a crew of drunken carpenters working in pitch darkness. Windows were broken, shakes missing, the front door hung precariously from a single hinge, and inside the stench of rotted food mingling with body odor was nauseating, though it did not appear to bother the permanent occupants in the slightest.

"This is the moost disgoosting place I've ever been in bar noone," asserted the chief.

He sat opposite Virgil, his hands tied behind his back.

"You talk funny, old man," drawled another, younger Claggett coming up to them.

"Don' he though, Asa?" said Virgil. "How comes it you

cain't speak 'murican proper, old boots?"

"The oonly thing moore disgoosting is the lot of you, you disreputoble scolliwogs, vermin, revolting sovages."

"What's your name, old boots?"

"Noone oov your blosted beeswox, pig face."

"You shouldn' oughta talk to Virge like that, Pop, you're liable to get yourself a rifle butt cross't the mouth."

Virgil thrust his hand into the chief's inside coat pocket, dug about, and brought out his billfold. He opened it to his I.D. card: PINKERTON NATIONAL above DETECTIVE AGENCY, centered by the human eye and the legend in quotes, "We never sleep." Virgil studied it, furrowing his brow. The chief brightened so he was hard pressed to hold back a smile. The man was obviously illiterate; he couldn't make out a word.

"What's this?"

"My identification."

"That's a eye."

"The eye of the Lord. Looking straight at you."

Virgil gulped slightly but perceptibly, slapped the billfold shut, and flung it into a small heap of garbage under assault by a squadron of flies in one corner.

Asa retrieved it and extracted the money. "Who are you? Whatta you do?"

"I'm an eye doctor," said Pinkerton. "My names is Ulysses Hayes," he added, combining the names of the current President and his predecessor.

Virgil grunted.

"Wot oorthly use could I possibly be tae you?"

"Maybe none, old boots, maybe we'd best blow you to bits here an' now an' drop your bones in the dry well. Soun' like a good idee to you?"

"Lemme kill him," pleaded an emaciated, wild-eyed man. He pulled a short-barreled, scroll-engraved Peacemaker from his belt and cocked it.

"Relax, Ephraim, we got better use for him alive than dead an' stinkin' up the well. Lemme tell you why we grabbed you, Mr. Eyeball. Our li'l brother, who is really only a chile, is a pris'ner o' the marshal back in town. What we're gonna do is offer to trade you for him. If the marshal goes for it, all well an' good. If he don't, if he don't think you're wuth Elon an' turns us down, you'd best plan on a visit to the well, savvy?"

"The marshal ond I scorcely know one anoother. Wot makes you think he'd wont tae swop him for me?"

"You better start hopin' an' prayin' that's just' what he'll do."

"We shoulda took the other one, Virge," said Ephraim, "the dude. He even ast to go. This ol' man ain' worth nothin' to nobody. Look at him, he's jus' a ol' tramp in borried clothes."

"He ain't no tramp nohow," burst Asa. "He's carryin' money. Tramps don' carry no money, do they, Virge, do they?"

"Shut up, Asa."

Ephraim still had his gun out and cocked. He knelt beside the chief and set the muzzle against his temple. "Feel that col', old man? Look at him, Virge, he's scared shitless."

"Is like hell. Come roun' front here an' look at his eyes. He ain' so much as blinkin'. He's a cool one even if he's ol' an' busted down. Put away your iron."

"You want tae rescue your yoonger broother, you say? Thon do so. It should be simple enough. You need oonly work oot a feasoble plon, mon, noot borrel into toon oll goons blazing like a boonch oov wild oborigines."

His words lowered Ephraim's gun, straightened him, and brought Asa and others over to where he and Virgil sat eye to eye.

"You gotta idee, Mr. Eyeball, let's hear it."

Raider groaned.
"Will you stop it."
"It hurts, goddamn it!"
He had been carried back to the hotel room on a discarded

window blind found amongst the trash in the alley alongside the Macomber Lodging House. His lean face was drawn with pain, but to Doc looking on there was as much disappointment in it as bodily discomfort. Both Pinkertons were still in a state of semi-shock inspired by the swift rush of events that followed the shot that had felled Raider.

Doc poured himself half a tumbler of whiskey and sat beside the bed, staring down into it in the manner of a tea leaf reader. "One thing is certain, we can't make a move until you're on your feet."

"Oh, bullshit. I can get up and walk aroun' good as you. And if I can do that I can sit a horse."

"You'll stay right where you are. All we need is for you to start bleeding again and stretch this whole mess out another additional week."

He drank, pondered further, and reached a decision. He rose from his chair.

"What are you doin'? Where you goin'?"

"Where do you think?"

"Not after the ol' man, not alone, Doc. You can't. I mean it. Without me to protect you you'll get shot to pieces. And him."

"I'm going to see Rhilander."

"What for? You think he'll help? Like hell, not after the way the chief brushed him off like so much lint. He won't give you the time o' day. Besides, he's all tied up with the Claggetts."

"And they've got the chief. All I'll do is offer to throw in with them. If we can rescue the chief we can finish off the Claggetts at the same time."

"The marshal's not interested in the chief, don'cha understand? He's prob'ly gettin' ready to ride out after 'em right this minute if he hasn't already."

"Possibly, but I can't believe he'd deliberately jeopardize the chief's safety by attacking the place."

"You still don't understand."

"What?"

"Doc, more likely than not *Rhilander doesn't even know they snatched him.*"

"Mmmm. You could be right."

"When you say it that way I know I am. They could blow their place apart and him inside with it. Maybe even set fire to it, you know, in retal, retal—tal—"

"Retaliation for their trying to burn up the office."

"Right. I say the best thing you can do is cross your fingers Rhilander hasn't left yet, get over there, and fill him in. Tell him, tell him—"

"I'll volunteer to help."

"Then come back and get me."

"Forget it."

"I mean it, Doc. If you don't I'll never forgive you. Cross my heart, hope to die. You help me downstairs and up on my horse and I'll be aces. Once I'm in the saddle I'll stay there. I can't open up the hole sittin' with my leg hangin' down so, can I? Can I?"

"Mmmmm."

"You're not listenin' to a word I'm sayin'!"

"I heard you. You're not going. Not a chance. I'd have to be an imbecile to help you get up on a horse." He moved to the door. "I'll be back, maybe. If I'm not, I'll be on my way out there with them."

"You son of a bitch! Come back here, Weatherbee! I'll beat you blue! Weatherbeeeeeeee!"

Doc found himself about thirty seconds and a hundred yards behind Marshal Rhilander and his deputies, who were riding hell-bent down the Williams road and out into open country. Had not the last man in the posse turned and noticed him, Rhilander and the others, numbering twenty in all, would not have slowed.

Doc came up beside him.

"We're in a hurry," said the marshal stonily. "What do you want?"

Doc told him about Allan Pinkerton's abduction.

Rhilander's expression refused to reflect so much as a glimmer of sympathy. "He wants to swap him for Elon," he said. "Not a chance."

"Not wait just a minute," said Doc testily.

"What for? Pinkerton's no concern of ours. All he has to do is keep his head down, he won't get hurt. He knows how to handle himself. He should."

"That's easy to say, Marshal, but where the Claggetts are involved you can't take anything for granted. You should know that better than anyone."

"I'll thank you not to tell me what I should know. Let's go, boys."

Doc laid a hand on his forearm and held it tightly. "Go ahead, but before you do I'll give you one last reminder. You're dealing with his life, that of a man who's a good deal more important to the country at large, to law enforcement, to important people than you or I or anyone in this territory. I warn you, Rhilander, if anything happens to him you'll be the one to answer for it. I'll see to it personally."

He released his arm and whirled about.

"Hold it, hold it. Don't go getting your tailfeathers in an uproar. I'm not mad that Pinkerton turned me down this afternoon. I was, maybe, but not now. Look, ride with us. Up here with me. By the time we get there, if you can come up with any bright ideas, I'll be willing to listen."

"Fair enough."

"Let's go."

Raider threw his good leg over the side of the bed and pushed himself up to a sitting position. "So far so good, leg."

Gingerly and slowly he brought his afflicted leg alongside it. Bending his knee and setting his foot on the floor tugged his wound slightly. It hurt, but he was sure it didn't open. He reached for the bottle left standing on the floor beside the chair. He took a healthy swig. What he needed was a crutch. No sooner did this thought cross his mind then he heard the door close next door.

"Hey! Hey, you out there. Come in here!"

He cocked his head and listened intently. All was quiet.

"Hey! Come in here! Quick! Matter o' life and death!"

The door flew open. There stood a chambermaid, her arms piled with dirty linen, her eyes wide with apprehension. She was well past middle age, her stringy gray hair hanging down, framing a face as plain as a pie pan, displaying a gloomy expression that bordered on downright suffering.

"Life and death?" she murmured caustically.

"I'm hurtin' bad, can'cha see? I got shot in the damn leg."

"I don't abide cussing."

"All right, all right. Listen, there's money in my pants pocket there, the left side. Take one dollar, go downstairs, and buy me a damn . . . a crutch."

"Only one?"

"I only got one bum leg, haven' I? Go to the general store, buy it, rent it, steal it, I don't care what, only get it back here pronto. And don't forget to bring back the change."

"Yes, Your Majesty. Will that be all, Your Majesty?"

"Hey, if I sound a little testy it's just 'cause it hurts. It isn't a damn . . . an hour old yet."

"Should you be walking on it so soon?"

"I won't be walkin', just gimpin'. Go get it, okay?"

She laid the dirty linen on the end of the bed and got a dollar out of his pocket.

"If the manager catches me sashaying out in the middle of my work he'll raise a ruckus. You'll have to explain it's an emergency."

"Yeah, yeah, don't worry about him."

She closed the door. He narrowed his eyes and grinned fiendishly. Utterby. He had him at last—as good as. All thanks to his suspicious imp. It was never to be ignored. There was something about that man. That "doctor." He hadn't thought about it the first time they'd met in the lobby,

but the second time in the restaurant window his imp had
whistled warning; something just wasn't right about him.
The suspicion formed in his gut, climbed his belly to his
throat and up into his brain, and sat there pulsing, demanding attention, thought, examining, pinpointing.

The single slender streak running down the doctor's right
cheek as he bent over him and dug out the slug was the
key. At that, he could barely make out his face through the
sweat dimming and burning his eyes, but when he blinked
rapidly and they cleared there it was: a streak. Like a tear
running through powder down a woman's cheek, only his
was sweat running through his makeup.

"He's a phony for sure!"

This conclusion was immediately followed by a blow
from a fist of ice that struck the top of his spine and sent
a chill rushing down it. He'd operated on him! In front of
half the town! Dug in his digger and dug out the slug! He
was no doctor. He didn't know a damn thing about taking
out a bullet! It had to be the first he'd ever tried! With him
the guinea pig! Of all the brass!

"His damn digger coulda been all dirty with germs. I
could be infected as a six-day carcass right this minute and
the hole closin' up, sealin' the germs inside sos they can
eat and eat and eat. Jesus! Bastard was no more a doctor
than Weatherbee, than the man in the friggin' moon, and
here he goes pokin' around and gougin' and diggin' like to
kill me helpless where I lay!

"Son of a bitch!"

He loosened the knot in his bandage so that he could lift
it sufficiently to be able to reach in and pull out the gauze
pad. It clung to the wound and had to be ripped loose, and
it hurt like hell when he did so. The hole was surrounded
by dried blood darkened by the carbolic acid Utterby had
used to sterilize it. Undiluted, it had burned the edges ragged
around the hole. Still, he was lucky: loosening the pad could
easily have started fresh blood oozing, but it had not. He
got out the roll of gauze Utterby had given Doc, tore off

six inches, and folded it into a fresh pad. Positioning it, he then resecured the knot.

He waited. He thought about Allan Pinkerton. Old Flasharity Weatherbee was dead right: the crotchety old pennypincher flailed him raw with his acid tongue, but in his miserable heart he did have a warm spot for him. Did care. Why did he? Maybe because underneath all the bullshit they were two peas from the same pod. They didn't have something in common, they had practically everything: both dirt poor, both struggling, battling often with their knuckles just to get from one day to the next, both short-tempered as hurt bulls, both impatient of stupidity, laziness, yellow guts, and faint hearts, all the things that separate the milk people from the bone people.

The Scot was a man and a half, the nasty son of a bitch: chasing and catching counterfeiters in his bare feet, battling four guys at he same time with his bare hands, shot at fifty times, stabbed, kicked, beaten helpless, left for dead on a Lake Michigan dock and in a loft in a barn in Dundee. Shot at so close his coat caught fire, two slugs shattering his forearm, plowing up to his elbow where the surgeon cut them out along with pieces of the cloth. Tough as an oak burl, only older now and since his stroke not well, never completely recovered from it. And that Claggett trash had to go and snatch him.

"Oh boy."

If they had any idea what they'd bitten off. He wouldn't take their guff, wouldn't blink. They threaten him he'd come back at them both barrels blasting. They'd wind up wishing to God they'd never laid eyes on him. Would they hurt him? They could. He'd reached a stage in his life where he talked a lot bigger threat than he posed. He might provoke them to break his bones out of pure orneriness, out of frustration or something. Hopefully, Rhilander, Doc, and the others would get a break, free him, and wipe out the pig family.

Hopefully.

Evening dragged forward. The chambermaid finally came

back with his crutch and 25 cents change.

"Good! Great! Terrific!" He snatched the crutch from her.

She gave him his change.

"Reach me my pants there, wouldja?" He pocketed the quarter, fished out a dime, and handed it to her. "For you, and thanks. I mean a ton. You've saved my bacon. You're some kinda woman."

"Joan of Arc, that's me."

She stared at the dime in her hand, sighed, pocketed it, picked up her dirty linen, and left. He set the rubber-knobbed crutch on the floor between his knees and slowly, deliberately, gritting his teeth, pulled himself to his feet. He felt no twinge, but when he slipped the crutch under his left arm and stepped forward pain struck like someone was poking a finger into the wound. When he shifted his weight to his sound right leg, however, it stopped.

He had never used a crutch before; he had to get the hang of it. Now that he thought about it, what was it but a substitute for his leg; there was really no need to touch the floor with his left foot. He practiced. He walked up the side of the bed, turned, came back down around the end and up the other side between his and Doc's bed. It wasn't hard, but his weight pressing down on the armrest threatened to set his armpit aching. He got out his bandanna and, balancing on one foot, tied it around the armrest, shoving the loose ends up under it for padding. Then he resumed practicing.

He could hear the chambermaid working in the room on the other side. He called her back, explained about the makeup case, and offered her a $10 reward if she found it.

"He's wanted for murder. You the only chambermaid in this dump?"

"There's Anna-Maria Valdez. She's Mexican. She and I take care of the whole place. We switch off floors, you know?"

"Yeah, I think her and I've met. Anyway, find that case

and I'll give you the ten."

"Ten dollars and ten cents. This is my lucky day."

Elmo Utterby studied his disguise in the mirror over the washbasin. The sweltering heat, its severity unabated even after sundown, drew sweat from his brow and sent it coursing down his face, rendering his disguise useless.

"You've a problem, old boy."

He double-checked the door to make certain he'd locked it, then returned to the mirror and stripped off his Van Dyke and mustache. The heat had softened the spirit gum and both came off easily. Too easily. Another twenty minutes in this heat and they'd likely have fallen off.

"That could be very embarrassing, Elmo."

He stripped to the waist and washed his face and neck thoroughly with soap. Then he got out the cord he had bought at the Merchandise Mart. He had followed a gray-haired lady up to the counter and waited while she ordered, of all things, one crutch. He was surprised the clerk was agreeable to selling her only one. Looping the free end of the cord around the makeup case, he opened the window and lowered the case to the trash heap below.

"Perfect!"

Knotting the cord at the proper length, he then hauled the case back up and cut the cord at the knot. He sat on the edge of the bed, flipping through his disguise booklet. He passed the old man's disguise he had employed earlier, paused, and went back to it.

"You did a good job on that one, old boy, though not as good and not as much fun as Dr. Feelgood. Not only did I diagnose Raider's nose, but I dug a bullet out of him. Under the worried eye of his partner no less." He got out the three dollars Doc had paid him. "Thank you again, Doc. Thank you both. Ah ha, ah ha, ha, ha, ha, ha, ha, ha!"

Darkness came swiftly, capturing and holding the suffocating heat of the day. Only a rainstorm would disperse it, but not a single cloud hung in the star-studded heavens. Marshal Rhilander, Doc, and the others drew near the Claggett spread. The house was in darkness. Under a three-quarter moon not a single horse could be seen. There was no sign of any life other than the peepers in the fields chorusing promise of another sweltering day tomorrow.

"Damn it!" burst Rhilander. "We're too late."

Deputy Rodwell came up on his other side. "They've gone back to town again, and taken Pinkerton with them. Rode cross country insteada the road."

"Could be. Send a couple of men over there to take a close look just to make sure. They might just be lying low, waiting to ambush us."

"No horses, Evan."

"Just do it, and tell them to keep down. Slip through the grass, see what they can see through the windows on either side."

They waited while the house was examined at close range. The two men came back to report it "as empty as a barrel."

"Let's get out of here," said the marshal.

"Wait," said Rodwell. "Before we go, why don't we leave our calling card. Burn the place down. We'd be doing the neighborhood a favor."

Doc privately disagreed, but said nothing; he'd seen the Claggetts in action; Raider was lying on a bed of pain thanks to them. But burning down their house . . . As Raider would say, it was getting even with your enemy behind his back. But Rhilander liked the idea. When he agreed to it, Doc shrugged his own objection off his conscience. After all, it was their war.

The house went up like tinder, lighting up the surrounding countryside a half mile in all directions. An enormous pillar of smoke rose from the blaze, blotting out the moon. They watched it briefly, feeling the heat against their cheeks, then the marshal signaled and away they rode.

Eleven riders rode nonchalantly toward town: Virgil, three of his brothers, six friends, and Allan Pinkerton, bestride a big-chested bay stallion. He rode alongside Virgil.

"I hope this idea works for your sake, Mr. Eyeball."

"It con't help boot work, Cloggett. Like oll my brain-children it's foolproof. You wont tae free your broother, this is the ontelligont way tae go aboot it."

Mortality appeared, squatting on the flat land like a brood hen, pricked here and there with yellow lights.

"We'll circle aroond ond coom oop oon the rear oov the marshal's oofice."

"You hear, boys?" said Virgil.

They drew within a hundred yards of the building. The rear was in darkness, but Ephraim, legging it down the alley along one side, came back to report lights burning in the office proper up front.

"We'll go in the froont door," said the chief. "You ond me, Cloggett."

"You mean just walk in?"

"Bold os bross, mon. I'll knock, you'll be richt behind me, your goon tae my bock. One false move on their part ond I'm a dead mon."

"You got yourself a pile o' guts for an old boots. You remind me of my pappy."

"I'm flottered," said Pinkerton dryly.

"The rest o' you boys spread yourselves round the place. Asa, you and the Willoughby brothers get out front. Ephraim, you'll be in charge outside here. Don' start no shootin' whilst we're in there. I don' fancy being trapped. Let's go. Man, I hope Rhilander's in there. Him I want."

"He ain't," said Ephraim. "I got a good look. They's just two men, leastwise in the office. Could be 'nother out back jawin' with Elon maybe."

"Damn."

"Let's nae be divorted froom oor main purpose, mon, the plon is tae rescue your broother. Rhilonder be dommed."

"Man's right, Virge," said Asa.

They dispersed. Virgil and Allan Pinkerton started down the alley, then came around front.

The chief approached the door. He raised his fist to knock,

then paused. "Raise your goon, mon. Point it to the bock oov my head."

"You said your back."

"The bock of my head's moore dromotic, nae? One false move oon their part ond you con blow my brains oot."

"Yeah..."

"Set you moozle against my skull. There you go."

He knocked. They could hear the door being unbolted top and bottom. It opened, and a single eye peered at them.

"What the hell..."

"Open up!" burst Virgil, setting his foot against the door and pushing. It flew wide. "Don' talk, just listen. This here's a swap—this ol'-timer for Elon. You agree and pronto, I mean in ten seconds, or I'll blow his brains out and kill you both. You there, stay clear o' the gun rack."

The two deputies slowly raised their hands.

"You're crazy, Virgil," said the younger deputy. "You'll never get away with it."

"Just watch. Elon... Elon!"

"Hey, Virge."

"You okay?"

"I want out."

"You got it, boy. Stan' apart, you two. Now slow-like unbuckle your belts and drop 'em. Do it!"

He cocked his gun. The chief stiffened and held his breath. Both men started to unbuckle.

"We can't swap you, Virgil, Evan'd kill us."

"If you don't, *I* will."

"We can't make no deal 'thout his say-so."

"Then this old man is dead and the two of you with him. Use your heads. I got the drop on you. The place is surrounded. I don't even have to make no deal; I could blast you all three and walk outta here with Elon. But I'm a' honorable man. I'll give you five seconds to spring him. One, two, three..."

Allan Pinkerton held his breath. He sucked in one last gasp, topping off his lungs, and with the swiftness of a rattler striking, doubled over, drove his right elbow backward with all the force he could muster, and at the same time stomped down his left boot, smashing Virgil in the toes. He howled and fired. The bullet flew over Pinkerton's back and lodged in the door separating the office from the cell area. The chief whirled and drove his fist into Virgil's midsection, doubling him. His gun tumbled from his hand. The deputies pounced on him. Two sharp blows to the back of the neck rendered him senseless.

"Guid work, lods. Noo pick him oop and stick him oot bock with his sibling. In seporate cells, mind you."

Marshal Rhilander, Doc, and the others came dusting into town, spreading out as soon as they reached the main street. They dismounted, tied up at various hitch racks, and assembled in the alley alongside the Macomber Lodging House.

"Mason, take a couple of men and get on down to the office. Check and see if the coast is clear."

"Right."

The others watched them start down the street toward the office, about 150 yards away. They moved slowly and carefully, approaching from both sides and concealing themselves in darkened doorways and behind pillars supporting overhangs as they moved.

A loud clumping sound came from behind Doc and the marshal, who turned their heads to see what it was.

"Oh my God."

"What the hell you gapin' at, Weatherbee? Never seen a man with a crutch before?"

Rhilander guffawed and slapped his knee.

Raider glared at him, his lip curling in a sneer. Then he grinned. "Guess what, Doc, I got Utterby fingered."

"I'm sure."

"I do. He's that doctor that dug the slug outta me." He explained.

"Is it possible?" asked Doc in an awed tone.

"It's him, damn it. He's somewheres around town, and I'm gonna find him. Gonna unmask him, pull the damn hair off his face, show him up for what he is, an embezzler. I'll track him down on a bone leg and a wood one and tie him up in a nice neat package with a blue ribbon around it for Hollenbeck and old A.P. Speaking of which, how come you're not out lookin' for him?"

"We think we've found him, Rade."

Raider looked about. "Where is he?"

"Down the street in my office," said the marshal. "The Claggetts took him."

"Then brought him back?" interposed Raider. "That's crazy."

Doc shook his head in disagreement. "He's not out at their place, none of them are. We figure they came back here. I wouldn't put it past the chief to have talked them into coming back. He—"

He stopped short, interrupted by a single muffled shot coming from up the street. Mason Rodwell and the others approaching the office also stopped. Gunfire erupted, coming out of the darkness around the office, attacking it from the alley and out front. Immediately, Rodwell and the others began firing. In seconds bedlam reigned.

"Oh my God," groaned Doc. "Here we go again. If he's inside there ... ."

"What are we waitin' for?" rasped Raider. "Let's go see."

"You stay put. You're in no condition to fight," said Doc.

"Let's go," said the marshal.

Off raced the lot of them, leaving Raider fuming, protesting, brandishing his crutch, completely ignoring the fact that it was supporting him and nearly falling down in consequence.

Allan Pinkerton sat with a two-week-old edition of the Phoenix *Sun & Intelligencer*. The two deputies were sitting on the floor, their guns in their laps, staring at him. Inside, Virgil had temporarily ceased bawling his empty threats in favor of turning his ire on his younger brother.

"What the hell you gotta go and get caught in the first place for, you pick-nose halfwit!"

"You got caught too. You got tricked. Least I got caught and arrested proper."

"Oh, shut your fool face! Hey, outside there, Mr. Eyeball, I'll get you for this, see iffn I don't! I'll tromp on your toes and elbow your gut fit to bust it, you old coot. I'll fix you proper!"

"Oh, shut up, Virge."

"You shut up, young-un."

"I see by the paper thot the Belinda mine stock is oxpected tae shoot oop tae the moon by the end oov the moonth."

"It's already shootin'," said the younger deputy, swiping his bright red hair from his eyes with his forehand. "It's goin' up every day. I got me four shares. I'm gonna be rich."

"Me too," said the other, a grizzled man in his early thirties with one eye slightly lower down his face than the other, which had peered through the partially opened door at the chief and Virgil earlier.

"Foosh, dinna poot your faith in pipe dreams. Ond poot your hard-earned moony into soomething oov soobstonce like hog futoors, the way I do."

Outside, the assault continued unabated. Occasionally a bullet would penetrate one or another wall only to spend itself driving through and drop harmlessly onto the floor. The two front windows and the single one looking out onto the alley alongside had long since been shattered. The door resembled a giant-sized upright slice of Swiss cheese, the upper panel in particular. Neither of the deputies nor the chief had suffered so much as a scratch.

"What are they shootin' at?" asked Red Hair.

"What do they ever?" responded Grizzled. "Those boys just love to shoot. They don't even care if they see what they're shootin' at. That's what makes 'em so dangerous."

"Foosh, richt noo they're aboot os dongerous os a blind mon locked in a bloody troonk. Hist, listen."

All three strained their ears. A second wave of shooting seemed to separate itself from the first, coming from out front. Red Hair crept across the floor and carefully sneaked a look out the corner of the front window.

"It's Mason Rodwell!" he exclaimed. "The marshal and the boys come back."

No sooner did he announce this unexpected turn then the Claggetts and their allies elected to abandon the fray. Seconds later they were mounted up and galloping out of town, leaving Virgil outraged and cursing his heart out in his cell.

"Ephraim, Asa, you bastards, you cowardly scum, come back here! You hear me? That's an order! Ephraim! Asa! Oh for Chrissakes!"

Pinkerton closed and folded the newspaper. "Well, lods, I guess thot's thot. Oonfosten the door, Deputy, ond let's give oor brave rescuers a royal welcoom."

CHAPTER NINE

By noon the next day every working chambermaid in Mortality had been alerted. Amazingly to Raider, Chief Pinkerton had raised the reward from $10 to Doc's $25. The three stood outside the bank. President Atherton waved greeting from within. In the window was posted the daily figures for both common and preferred Big Bonanza Company stock. Preferred had jumped to $56 a share in two days. Common had inched up from $38 to $40. An air of celebration permeated the town, evidenced by everyone's smiles, gay laughter, and all-around good feeling.

Allan Pinkerton, however, was not smiling. "It grieves me tae the quick tae hov tae desert you two in the middle oov the case, boot dooty colls in Chicago. Os capable os Will Wogner ond my sor.s are, they con't seem tae roon the oofice withoot me. 'Twas ever thoos. I've read thot Rome nearly collopsed whenevor Joolius Caesor took a vacation."

"We'll miss you," said Raider dryly.

"Like you'd miss consomption," retorted the chief. "Ne-

83

vortheless, oof I go. The plon is in the works, ond if, os you claim, Raider, you've fingered the occused os your ottending physician, you've a leg oop oon the roscal."

"Unfortunately, he's most certainly changed his disguise again by now," said Doc wearily.

"Ah, boot you've booth seen him, disguised though he wos. You've booth seen his wolk, stonce, gestoors, etcetera, etcetera. A capoble ooperative, one with booth eyes oopen ot oll times, perceives the little things. Raider's oonmosking him con nae boot holp."

"Let's hope," said Doc.

His eyes went to Raider's. He had never seen him so anxious to get rid of anybody. He quelled a chuckle.

"One thing strikes me os curious," said Pinkerton. "This businoss oov his honging aboot toon. Why does he? He could hie himself oof tae Timbooctu ond still coolect on his investmont."

"I think he absolutely revels in playing his game with us," said Doc. "It's a histrionic tour de force. It must do wonders for his vanity. He's managed to stay one disguise ahead of us so far. I'd be amazed if he left."

"He'll leave if he decides you're cloosing in on him."

"Good point."

"Hurry things oop, lods. Mr. Hollenbock ond the S.P. are hoving cooniption fits oover this mess. Ond you, Raider, take care oov yourself. Dinna ooverdo the godding aboot. Your partnor'll need you fit os a fiddle when the showdown rolls aroond."

"Yeah, yeah."

Pinkerton climbed aboard his rented fly, saluted them, slapped rump, and trundled off. Raider sighed the sigh of a doomed man reprieved from the firing squad just as the order to aim was given.

"What now?"

Doc shrugged. "I don't see as there's anything we can do until one of the chambermaids gets back to us."

"Which could be weeks, and maybe never."

"I doubt that. We know he's in town. We know he's staying at one of the six hotels."

"We know he was. He coulda moved into a private place overnight. He coulda, you know, coulda even left town."

"That's my boy—pile on all the optimism. Let's go get a drink."

Speculating on the fugitive's movements proved very nearly prophetic on Raider's part. Upon arising that morning, Elmo Utterby began to seriously consider giving up his room in the Macomber—not for one in another hotel, but a private residence. Further thinking on this possibility, however, betrayed possible flaws. Coming and going in a hotel was easy. He was casually observed if at all. Rooming in a private home would fix the landlady's attention on him and keep it there. Also, it would be easy for her to go through his room in his absence. In a hotel only the chambermaid was permitted to enter.

The convenience of the trash heap under his window for hiding his makeup case emboldened him to stay put at the Macomber. Strolling about town in his new disguise, he studied the exterior walls of all five of the other hostelries and determined that his hiding place could not be duplicated. To be sure, the trash heap wasn't the only place to hide the case, but it did appear the safest.

He had changed into the disguise of a nondescript-looking middle-aged man with a straw hat and the same outfit he had worn as the old man. The lower half of his face was normally wedge-shaped. He had skillfully rounded it by painting on jowls and a double chin. He also reduced the width of his mouth by raising his upper and lowering his lower lips. The overall effect was startling. He now had an almost perfectly round face, and by adding a handlebar mustache he had made himself look totally different from his normal appearance and all his previous disguises.

"You're a genius, Elmo, old boy."

He was in luck. Overnight the heat wave passed and a

cooling breeze came wafting down from the Conconino plateau to the north. He need have no further worry about perspiration betraying his makeup.

He stopped in front of the bank window seconds after Raider and Doc said their goodbyes to the chief and walked and limped off. President Atherton came to the door chewing a nougat square. He hailed him as he stood reading the stock figures posted on the glass.

"Every day sees her climb another notch. Can I interest you in purchasing a few shares, brother?"

"No tanks," he replied in an accent that could have been anything from Finnish to Yugoslavian. "I don't kamble."

"This is no gamble, friend, this is investing. The fuel that powers the machine of free enterprise, sir. It's what made and is making America great."

"Tank you, but I don't tink so. Cood day."

By the time Raider and Doc got to the Macomber, Raider was in poor shape. He had obviously overdone it.

"You shouldn't even be trying to walk this early."

"I know what I can do and what I can't, Weatherbee. I don't need any nursemaid. I sure don't need you."

"Why don't you go back to the room and go to bed."

"I just decided to, but not 'cause you say so. I can make up my own mind. I can, you know."

"Need any help?"

"No!"

"I'll be back in a little bit. I'm somewhat tired from last night myself, and I could use a nap. See you later."

He waved and mounted the steps. A comely young lady with flashing eyes and a lovely smile was on the desk. Doc moved to tip his derby, for the moment forgetting that it and the hole through it had been disposed of and he was now bareheaded. He introduced himself and showed her his I.D. She was visibly impressed.

"We're after a fugitive. He came down from San Francisco, and we tracked him to Mortality. He's resorting to all sorts of disguises. He's very clever and talented."

He proceeded to describe the doctor. She listened, pursing her lips, her eyes downcast on the register book. When he was done she flipped the pages.

"Two C. It's just down the center of the lobby."

Doc's heart quickened. "You recognize him?"

She nodded. "It's really strange. I have no idea what name he registered with, not a clue as to what he really looks like. I had two days off. I went to visit my sister and her husband in Flagstaff."

"Yes, yes."

"Very strange."

"What?"

"Recognizing his disguise, but not recognizing him, not knowing him if I fell over him. I was coming down from the third floor last evening. He came down behind me. The doctor. He looked exactly like you describe him."

"Two C, you say."

She nodded. "I didn't actually see him come out the door, but that has to be it."

"Why do you say that?"

"There are only four rooms at the front, and I know who's registered in the other three." She went back to the register. "Let's see . . ."

"No, it's all right. That's good enough for me. Thank you, miss. Thank you very, very much."

She tittered. "You're welcome, I'm sure."

"Is he in now, do you know?"

She glanced at the pigeonholes behind her. "No key."

"Could you let me in? I'd like to take a look around."

"I—"

"I'd only be a minute or two. I could get a court order, but it'd save me a lot of time if . . ."

She had lowered her head. She lowered her voice. "I guess it'll be okay." She got a key out of the drawer in front of her. "Please bring it straight back, and don't forget to lock the door when you leave, and try not to let anybody see you go in, and don't disturb anything."

"I'll be very careful. I promise. Thank you, thank you."

She beamed. "You're cute. I love your suit."

"Thank you."

He started up the stairs two at a time, then slowed his step, not wanting to appear conspicuous. He hesitated in front of 2C. It was possible Utterby was inside and was merely carrying his key around with him, not returning it until he checked out. He pressed his ear against the door and listened. He could hear nothing. He unlocked the door and went in. The bedclothes were rumpled; nothing else was in disarray. He sniffed, hoping to catch the scent of greasepaint or powder, but there was none. He checked under the bed. There was nothing but dust bunnies. He went through the bureau drawers. Nothing suspicious. He checked under the pillow, then the mattress, not knowing why he bothered, just being thorough. Then too, it was possible Utterby had rid himself of the case and squirreled the contents away in several different places. Possible, but unlikely. He checked behind the bureau and under it. He went to the window. There was nothing on the ledge.

He started on the closet. Among the clothes was a suit that looked quite like the doctor's, but he couldn't be altogether sure. There was a pair of kid button shoes, and rubber-soled slippers. There was also a suitcase. It was empty.

He checked the overhead shelf. There was a shoe box. He glanced at it and away. It was too small to hold the makeup case. He was about to close the door on it when he changed his mind. No harm in checking it out. He got it down and undid the string around it. Inside was something soft wrapped in butcher's paper and tied with another string lengthwise and sidewise. Taking care not to tear the paper, he unwrapped it.

His heart jumped in his chest so that for a fleeting instant he imagined it had pulled loose from its moorings. All told the stock certificates totaled 1,800 shares. If Utterby had bought them for $50 a share two days before, he'd already realized over $10,000 in paper profit.

Rewrapping them, he put them back in their box and tucked the box under his arm. Until they caught up with Elmo they would hang on to his ill-gotten gains. If nothing else, the certificates would serve as insurance against his leaving town.

"Now, Elmo, the shoe is on the other foot." He grinned at the mirror. "Now you can start looking for us for a change."

CHAPTER TEN

Not five minutes after Doc returned the passkey to the lady behind the desk and departed the Macomber Lodging House the occupant of 2C returned to his room carrying a brand new scroll-barreled Eagle-Butt Peacemaker .45 with a mother-of-pearl grip displaying dollar signs on either side. His ever dependable instincts had sternly advised him to procure a gun; the dollar sign emblems seemed to suit his chosen occupation. Along with the gun he purchased two boxes of cartridges.

He brought back as well his decision to leave Mortality. He would return to San Francisco; he was homesick, though he gave no thought whatsoever to returning to his apartment on Market Street. No, he'd find a new place, perhaps on Monterey Boulevard; he liked Mount Davison Park. He could grow a beard and hide behind it for the rest of his life. The months and years would roll by, and in time Hollenbeck and the Southern Pacific would forget about Elmo Utterby. The loss would be written off, if it hadn't been already, and the incident would slip into the history of the company. If his holdings in the Big Bonanza Company continued to appreciate at anywhere near their current pace, say for the next year, they could double, perhaps even triple in value. He would sell out, take the money, and diversify. Perhaps sell only half the stock. Whatever he decided, the future promised a lucrative life of ease.

He sat on the edge of the bed holding his gun in the manner of one contemplating suicide; such a self-inflicted fate was the furthest thing from his mind, however. He thought about Wilfred Trimble, his assistant, the father of the twin boys. He thought about the company's refusal to grant Trimble a raise and the night he'd dropped the $1,000 through his bedroom window. The next morning Trimble had come to him in a state of near apoplexy, so excited was he. He told him about the money; he couldn't imagine who had given it to him. He kept repeating "it's like it dropped out of the sky." Of course Utterby hadn't told him the truth; no need.

He couldn't begin to describe the look on his face; on second thought he could: three parts relief, two parts pure, unrestrained, absolute joy. How it had warmed his heart to see him! He missed Trimble, missed everyone in the office. He did not miss E.S. Hollenbeck or J.B. Cantor or the rest of the brass. He wondered how the twins were faring, wondered how the books were since they had passed into the hands of his successor. He wondered if Trimble had been given his job. He was entitled to it, and was next in line.

He lit a stogie and puffed. He got up, took off his coat, and hung it in the closet. He was about to close the door when something prompted him to lift his eyes to the shelf. It was empty. Again he moved to close the door.

"Empty!"

He blanched. His eyes bulged from his head. He elevated himself on his toes and foolishly, futilely fumbled his hands across the bare shelf.

"Damn! Those damned Pinkertons!"

He began to curse uncharacteristically. He got control of himself, snatched up his pistol, and began to load it. His hands shook as he fumbled cartridges into the chambers.

Doc was right, Raider thought, he had overdone it. His leg from his knee up to the point of his hip ached furiously. And centering the discomfort was the hole under the gauze pad. It was already beginning to knit, and there was no sign of infection, but it hurt. It was soooo sore, like someone was poking a rod into it and twisting it about. It needed rest; he did too.

He lay on the bed staring at the ceiling, weighing the situation up to this point. Doc was also right about approaching the desk clerk at the Macomber. The three of them had seen the doctor come down the stairs bag in hand. At the time they'd naturally assumed he was visiting a guest patient; it hadn't occurred to them that he himself was a guest. But now that they knew without any doubt that he was a phony, that he was in fact Elmo, it followed that he must be registered there. Why they hadn't run there and checked with the desk first thing in the morning was beyond him. Doc would probably be too late now; Utterby had to have flown that coop for another.

A knock.

"Yeah?"

"It's the manager, Mr. Raider. Telegram for you."

"Oh for Chrissakes, he hasn't been gone an hour and already he's jabbin' back at us. What a damn pest that man is! Shove it under the door."

"You have to sign for it."

"Okay, okay, the door's unlocked."

It slammed open. There stood a man with a straw hat and handlebar mustaches snaking across his round face. Rage fired his eyes. He slammed the door behind him and pulled a gun.

"On your feet!"

"What the hell! Who—"

"You heard. Up!"

"I can't, I'm hurtin', I got shot in the leg. A damn butcher dug the slug out. Come within a whisker o' stabbin' me to death."

"Get up or I'll kill you where you lay."

"All right, all right, all right. Jesus Christ, you don't have to get nasty about it."

He stood, supported by his crutch.

"Now get 'em out. You've got ten seconds."

"What?"

"Don't start playing games. I'll kill you, so help me. My certificates, hand 'em over."

"You . . . you're him! Utterby!"

"You're wasting time." He cocked and two-handed the gun, raising it to the level of Raider's chest.

"Take it easy with that thing. I haven't got 'em, I swear. What the hell makes you think I do?"

Utterby glanced about. "Raider . . ."

"I'm tellin' you the truth, I haven't even seen 'em."

"You're a liar."

"Like hell."

Utterby lowered the gun slowly; he stood pondering, sustaining his fury, his eyes fierce. He looked about, then began to search, whipping open the bureau drawers, running his free hand through their contents, searching the closet from the overhead shelf down. He came back to where Raider stood beside the bed.

"Stand clear."

He upended the mattress. There was nothing underneath. Giving it up, he confronted Raider. He jabbed the gun against his midriff.

"For the last time . . ."

"I'm tellin' you I don't know what the hell you're talkin' about! Oh, I know about the stocks. What I mean is they're not here. You can see that. You got it all screwed up, man."

"Let's go."

"I can't, I'm a invalid, I can't walk hardly."

Utterby tossed Raider his Stetson. "Put it on. We're leaving. I don't want to kill you here. We'll go downstairs and out back. You're going to die in privacy."

"You're crazy as a hoot owl."

"Move."

Doc was in no hurry to get back to the hotel with his prize. Leaving the Macomber, he thought about what he should do with the certificates. He certainly couldn't carry them around. Put them in the bank for safekeeping? It was a possibility. Put them in the hotel safe? Either was preferable to burying them in the ground. Maybe Raider would have an inspired idea. He usually did. For an uneducated man, one whom some of the agency's operatives suspected of treading dangerously close to downright illiteracy—though Doc himself was not one of them—the plowboy was surprisingly inventive. He had a positively remarkable sense of logic. Time and again he saw the problem clearly and the best, often the only, solution. Witness his idea of searching for Utterby's makeup case rather than Utterby. It had led to the certificates. And they in turn could force the fugitive's hand.

The shoe box under his arm, he walked by the bank. Eustace Atherton was just coming out. He hailed Doc.

"Guess what? Word's just come in—there's been a tremendous strike out at the Belinda."

"You don't say."

"Fantastic! Shares have jumped to nearly three times this morning's value." He waggled a fat finger reprovingly. "I warned you two to get in on it. Ten little shares would be worth fifteen hundred now. It wouldn't be unwise to buy even now. They've no place to go but up."

Doc did some speedy mental calculation. Utterby's stock under his arm was now worth in excess of a quarter of a million. Amazing.

"They found a vein as wide as a barn door. The engineer reports it appears to go halfway back to Government Mountain. It's the richest strike in history. Makes the Comstock

Lode look like nickels and dimes." He chortled and rubbed his hands. "What a glorious day! What a wonderful life! We're all rich, rich, rich!"

"Congratulations," Doc murmured and walked on.

He mounted the stairs two at a time. He knocked on the door, then opened it. And gasped. The place looked as if it had been turned upside down.

"Rade..."

He sprinted back down to the lobby. The desk clerk who doubled as a counterman at the Merchandise Mart was on duty, pushing mail into the pigeonholes.

"Have you seen my partner?"

"Sure. He came in about forty minutes ago. He's up-stairs."

"No he's not."

"He didn't go out again, I would have seen him. Would have heard him with that crutch of his. It sounds like a trip-hammer."

"He's not in his room. Is there a back way out?"

"Yeah. Is something wrong, do you think?"

"How do I get there?"

"Go back upstairs. There's a door right in front of you. It leads to the back stairs and down to the backyard."

Doc waved thanks and raced up the stairs. By the time he got to the back stairs door he had his .38 Diamondback out, checking to make sure it was loaded. It was. When he reached for the doorknob the shoe box slipped from under his arm. He retrieved it, jerked open the door, and ran down the stairs. At the back door he paused and looked from side to side through the window. No sign of anyone.

Outside he ran to his left, pulling up short at the corner of the building. He could hear voices.

"You're not gonna plug me, you know you're not."

"You're wrong. I've put too much into this thing to see it all go down the drain. If they catch me I'll go to jail for twenty years as it is. Hollenbeck'll see to it. They might as well hang me."

"Stealin's one thing, murder's somethin' else."

"I don't care. I'll be a lot better off with you out of the way. And your sidekick. Say your prayers."

Doc whirled around the corner and let fly with a shot—but too soon, before he was able to stop his momentum. The shot flew by the brim of Utterby's straw hat. He reacted, turning his gun on Doc, but before he could fire Raider, who was down on his knees, preparing to meet his Maker, lunged, knocking him off balance. Lead bit into the corner post inches above Doc's head. He pulled back to cover.

"Give it up, Utterby, it's all over!"

"Doc . . . Doc . . ."

Doc lowered to a crouch and slowly, tentatively peered around the corner. Utterby had fled. Raider was down on hands and knees groping for his fallen crutch.

"Chrissakes, get after the son of a bitch!"

Doc raced past him toward the street end of the alley. "Where'd he go?"

"How in hell do I know? You think I can see through solid buildin's? You're an idiot, you know that, Weatherbee!"

There was no sign of Utterby. Doc jammed his gun into his belt.

"You all right?"

"Course I am! Jesus Christ, did you have to let him get away?"

"He's quick, Rade."

"You had him dead bang." He glowered. "You gonna stand there breathin' or you goin' after him?"

"I don't think he's going far." He held up the shoe box in the manner of a crown being offered to a king. "Not without his certificates."

"Big deal. We still gotta catch him. Go get the horses. Move!"

Upon leaving the alley, Utterby did what every resource-ful and desperate fugitive does: stole the first horse he came upon. Jumping into the saddle, he galloped off down the

Williams road. He glanced back; they weren't following yet. Raider's leg would slow them. Knowing the two of them as he had come to recently, they would squander time arguing whether Raider should come along or not.

So it was the other one who'd pilfered his stocks after all. He wasn't surprised. After searching their room and finding no trace of them and reading the surprised look on Raider's face as authentic, he suspected he'd caught up with the wrong man. He wouldn't have killed him; Raider didn't know that, but he wouldn't have. It couldn't hurt his cause to kill both, but he'd never be able to do such a thing, save perhaps in self-defense.

The land stretched before him, dominated by high mountains, gashed with superb canyons of rivers, laced with dry gullies and washes; the beds of intermittent streams, varied with great shallow basins, sunken deserts, dreary levels, imposing buttes, picturesque mesas, scattered forests, and rare verdant valleys turned golden brown under the summer sun.

Far ahead, upwards of a hundred miles, stretched the Grand Canyon. He saw no need to ride that far to escape his pursuers. In a couple of miles he would circle back, find a spot to rest, idle away the rest of the day, and return to town that night. Sneak back into the American the back way up to their room and surprise them. With any luck they'd still have the shoe box. Once he'd retrieved it he'd get out. And head where? Back to San Francisco? Not right away. And he didn't have to decide right away. With close to $3,000 he could go anywhere.

"Only not without the certificates, old boy."

He slowed his horse and cast a look back. He saw no one and no dust in the distance. To his left a barn and the charred remains of a house were visible. A number of men milled about the front of the barn. He got the impression that, having lost the house, they were living in the barn. He counted seven. They waved as he passed. He waved back. Fifty yards beyond he pulled up. The horse snorted, shook its head, and pawed the ground. He turned about and went slowly back. An idea was forming. He suspected that the Pinkertons had not started after him because they had gone to the marshal for help. They knew he was armed. Raider in his present condition was all but useless. He probably couldn't even sit a horse. Doc could and was armed, but he may very well have decided that one chasing one wasn't to his liking.

He saw two choices: keep riding and hide out the best place he could find, which meant giving up on recovering the certificates for the time being at least, or go back to town with help and if necessary take back the certificates by force.

"Howdy," said Ephraim.

Utterby introduced himself as Mr. Watson. Ephraim introduced himself, Asa, and the others.

"I'd like to hire you men."

"Hire?" Ephraim frowned. "Us? Sorry, stranger, we don't work for folks. Couldn't if we did. We got our hands full right now."

"How many are you?"

"Eight, but—"

"I'll pay a hundred dollars apiece."

"Hunnert..." Asa's eyes bugged. Ephraim too looked surprised.

"To protect me."

"'gainst what?"

"Two Pinkertons in town. They're out to kill me."

"What for?"

"Who knows? They've evidently got me confused with somebody else. I just got away from them by the skin of my teeth. They stole a shoe box from me. Help me get it back and I'll give you another hundred bonus."

"Two hunnert dollars!" boomed Asa.

"What's in the shoe box?" Ephraim asked. "Money?"

"My medication. I've a bad heart; it keeps me alive. They want me dead so they deliberately stole it. Ever hear of anything so cruel in your life? If I don't get it back within twenty-four hours I'm a dead man."

"We'll help you," said Asa eagerly. "For two hunnert bucks."

"Not so fast," said Ephraim. "I'm still the leader, young-un. We got a job of our own to do tonight," he added, looking back at Utterby. "Got to spring two men from the jail. We got a plan."

"Tell him, Ephraim," urged Asa. "It's my plan. We're gonna run a wagonload o' hay into town, smack up to the marshal's office, light it afire, and whilest the front is bur-nin' away and them inside are runnin' for their lives, we bust in the back and get out the boys. How's that for a plan? Is that great shucks or not?"

"Shut up, Asa, you talk too much."

"We could be all wound up with my problem long before nightfall if we get a move on," said Utterby.

He got out his wallet and passed out seven one-hundred-dollar bills to Ephraim, Asa, and the others, and one more to a runty little man with a hat much too large for him who came out of the barn.

"You got a plan?" asked Ephraim.

"We'll head into town. I'll precede you by a hundred yards or so. When I see them I'll give you the high sign."

"Wait, wait, wait," interjected Ephraim. "That's no good. We can't go back into town in broad daylight."

"You must."

"We can't. We wouldn't get two yards down the street."

"We'd get blowed to kingdom come," asserted Asa.

Utterby was about to offer argument when he raised his eyes and saw a dust pillar a mile or more distant. "It's them! Inside the barn, quick!" He bustled them inside, horses and all, and took up a position by one partially opened door.

"They seen us," said Ephraim.

"If they did they're not slowing down. Maybe they're too busy arguing to notice. You boys find slits and knot-holes. When they come by, shoot to kill. A hundred extra bonus on top of the other half to the ones who kill them!"

• • •

"This gotta be stupider than your usual stupidness," growled Raider. "We shoulda grabbed the first two horses we saw. Bet your boots he did. But no, you gotta play it straight, Mr. Sportsmanship, and go get ours. He's gotta be ten miles away by now."

"I don't care if he's fifty, Rade, he'll be back."

"If you're so sure o' that, what are we doin' chasin' him?"

They were about a quarter mile from the barn. Doc recognized it and the rubble of the house beyond.

"That's the Claggetts' place, what's left of it."

"Slow down."

"What for?"

"Pull up."

"Rade . . ."

"Do like I say, for Chrissakes." They stopped. "That barn's a perfect ambush."

"Don't be ridiculous. The Claggetts aren't the least bit interested in us."

"I'm talkin' about Utterby. Think about it. He had to come out this road; he's likely still on it. It's flat as your hand four or five miles straight ahead between those two buttes. You don't see any dust. You don't see anywhere he coulda turned off. That buncha trash lit out from the office last night. They had to ride someplace. He hadda pass by the barn there."

A shot whistled by his right shoulder.

"My God," murmured Doc.

"What'd I tell you? Was I right or was I right? How 'bout that for brains!"

They had swung about and were galloping back down the road. Fifty yards down Raider again pulled up.

"Let's get us behind that ledge there."

Doc glanced back at the barn. Men were piling out shooting wildly. Lead whined all around them.

"Damn!"

They downed their horses and threw themselves behind cover. Raider grunted in pain.

"Friggin' leg, friggin' Utterby, friggin' A.P., friggin' life!"

"Speaking of which, you neglected to thank me for saving yours."

"Big deal. I'm still fifty or sixty up on you. I wish we had a rifle."

"Here they come."

The outlaws were fanning out, some dropping to one knee to brace their weapons with their elbows before firing. Two flopped down on their bellies. There were no boulders, no hillocks, nothing for them to hide behind until one came upon a gully. A lone figure stood in the doorway of the barn.

"Get a load of old Elmo," growled Raider. "He stands back and watches them do his dirty work for him."

Doc fired. His target jumped, yelled, clutched his chest, and went down.

"Open the good eye, lucky britches."

The attackers were now widening the fan, suggesting they intended to circle them, or at least get far enough around to render the ledge useless as cover. They continued to pin them down with well-aimed rifle fire. Raider had emptied his gun. He began to reload. Doc too began to reload.

"What are you doin'? Don'cha know enough to measure out your shootin'? Us both reloadin' together gives 'em a chance to move up, for Chrissakes! Look. See?"

"I'm sorry, I'm sorry."

Raider loaded three shells and resumed firing. The third shot got the man closest to them in the forehead. His head snapped back like he'd run full tilt into a crossbeam.

"Two down."

Hostilities continued for fully ten minutes without letup. Both Pinkertons wounded men, and neither one sustained any wounds himself, but their supply of ammunition was dwindling rapidly.

"We can't get stuck here with empties, Doc, they'll cut us down like so much barley."

"What do you suggest?"

"Make a run for it. Head straight back, ziggin', zaggin', and prayin'."

"I don't know, Rade."

"I do! It's either that or wind up throwin' rocks at 'em. Look over to your left there—that clown in the gully's closest. The rest haven't moved a foot in a long time. Concentrate on him. Watch him. He raises up every so often. We knock him out, the rest are far enough away so we can get clear."

"I don't know, Rade."

"Will you stop sayin' that! If you'da potted him back in the alley, we wouldn't be in this fix now!"

"If you hadn't foolishly taken a shot at one of them you wouldn't have gotten hit in retaliation."

"Oh shut up. Look there, see? He raised up. Next time he does, let him have it. Move over a few yards, we'll catch him in a crossfire."

Doc did so. Both stared rapt at the gully and waited and waited while bullets flew all around them. Suddenly a hat shot up, a head, shoulders. They fired. The hat flew off; the head fell to one side.

"Good boy! Let's go."

"What about Utterby?"

"Screw him, he's second; first come our butts!"

They pulled their horses upright. Raider mounted with difficulty, grimacing. Off they flew flat in the saddle and zigzagging, followed by a spirited volley. Raider got out ahead and stayed there. Presently he slowed, then stopped; Doc came up alongside. He was examining his right shoulder. A shot had ripped through the padding of his coat.

"Eighty-two dollars."

"Let's circle round behind that rise over there. Maybe we can get back to the barn before they do. Get the drop on Utterby and take him."

They rode like the wind, circling a sprawling rise festooned with mesquite and supporting a small army of giant cactus. It was better than fifteen minutes before the rear of the barn thrust itself darkly and starkly into view. Without breaking stride they galloped up to it, separating, thundering down the sides to the front. There was no sign of Utterby or his horse. Raider rode inside.

"Nothin' but hay and stink. Let's get outta here."

Doc glanced toward the battlefield. They would be well advised to "get outta" there. The outlaws had regrouped and evidently stopped to tend to their dead and wounded and discuss the situation. Spotting Doc, they were now coming fast. Raider emerged, took one look, slapped haunch, and dug in his heels, yelping in pain as he did so. Off they rode down the side of the barn and onto their approach route.

"Son of a bitch! Son of a bitch!"

"They won't come after us, Rade, they can't be bothered."

"It's not that, it's my hole. It's opened up; I can feel it warm and wet. Wouldn't you know!"

"Does it surprise you?"

"Do I sound it? Can't you tell mad from surprised for Chrissakes!"

"You've done everything but twist your leg behind your neck. It's bound to open. You want to stop?"

"Oh hell yes, give them a fightin' chance to catch up."

"I'll take care of your wound back at the hotel."

"You don't touch it. I'd rather Utterby than you. The road's on the other side o' that hill. Let's get on it. We can move twice as fast."

Raider's crutch still lay where he'd dropped it in the alley when Doc brought him his horse. He reclaimed the crutch and together they mounted the backstairs to the room.

"Lie down, I'll pull down your pants and we'll have a look."

To Doc's surprise Raider made no protest. His wound had indeed reopened, but the blood oozing from it was dark, clear, and healthy-looking; no sign of infection. Doc stanched it with a fresh pad and rebandaged it.

"You take it easy."

"Where you goin'?"

"Downstairs to the desk. In our hurry to get after Utterby I simply handed the shoe box to the clerk and told him to stash it in the hotel safe for a while. Temporarily. I want to make sure it's still there."

"I'm coming."

"Don't be a ninny."

Doc fled. He pounded down the stairs to the front desk. The clerk with the slicked-down hair and the second job was still on duty. He appeared to be in a trance. He was white-faced and sweating; Doc thought he discerned him trembling but couldn't be certain. Whether he was or not, something was definitely amiss.

"What happened?" he rasped.

"Fellow came in. Not two minutes ago. I was alone. Not a soul in the lobby."

"What happened?"

"He pulled a gun. Threatened to kill me. Demanded I give him your shoe box."

"Oh Lord."

"How could he know you gave it to me?"

"A logical assumption. On the part of a logical man. I was either carrying it with me or I'd left it someplace. 'Someplace' would have to be the hotel safe. I wouldn't waste time running up to the room, and the box wouldn't be as safe there. He simply put two and two together."

"He scared the life out of me. His eyes . . . I was petrified he'd pull the trigger."

"You didn't see which way he went when he left. You couldn't have."

"I didn't see a blessed thing; I just sat down and tried my best to stop shaking and get hold of myself."

"He didn't go out the Williams road, we came in that way. We would have caught up with him, would have at least seen his dust. Where does the north road lead?"

"Red Lake, but he could cut off into the mountains before there, the San Franciscos."

"He could cut in any direction. By now he may even have doubled back, circled town, and is heading south."

"I'm sorry about the box."

"It wasn't your fault. It was ours for circling so wide, giving him time to get away." The clerk didn't quite understand. "Never mind," Doc added.

CHAPTER ELEVEN

Doc debated whether or not to go back upstairs. Raider would hit the ceiling when he heard, which wouldn't do his condition any good. He was just as much at fault, but by twisting logic he'd find some way to heap the lion's share of blame on his partner's shoulders. Allan Pinkerton was the one Doc worried about. When the chief left town they were closing in on Utterby; it actually did seem "only a matter of time." They had closed in and gotten a firm hold on his Achilles heel—the certificates—only to let him and them get away.

Three hundred and sixty degrees, three hundred and sixty escape routes. Take your pick, Elmo.

Doc sat in the lobby, drawing on an Old Virginia cheroot, drumming his fingers against the arm. He was deep in thought. If he were Utterby, where would he flee to? Talking further with the clerk established that Red Lake was only a leisurely ten-minute ride to the north. It was as good a place as any to start. The picture wasn't completely black. Utterby *had* gotten away with the certificates and enough cash to travel far and wide, but with only the clothes on his back, leaving his makeup case and with it any future disguises he might have planned. He couldn't replace the case in a place like Red Lake. He probably couldn't replace it anywhere in the territory, save Phoenix or Tucson.

"Phoenix? Tucson?" They could telegraph the law to be on the lookout for him in both places.

He tugged on his cheroot, then stumped it out in the potted palm at his elbow. Utterby's makeup case had been his salvation. His skillful use of the contents had enabled him to dupe them completely for days. With it he rode high; without it he was just another fugitive on the run, peering back over his shoulder. Were he Utterby, the very first thing he'd do would be to replace the case.

"Of course!"

And to do that he'd have to ride to Phoenix or Tucson, Phoenix being the closer. A loud clumping drew his attention to the stairs.

Raider appeared. "What the hell you doin', snoozin'?"

"Sit."

Doc related the bad news, following up with his conclusion regarding Utterby's makeup case. Raider agreed that he'd have to replace it. But then proceeded to add another dimension to the theory.

"Or get back his old one."

"How can he do that?"

"How would you? I know how I would. I'd come back here, stop off, and pick up the shoe box like he did and ride on out. You know, just to throw us off the trail."

"Why bother riding on out if we're not right behind him?"

"In case he's spotted pickin' up the box and whoever sees him tells us. Then when I get outta town I'd circle back and get the makeup case."

"He doesn't keep it in his room, Rade. I know, I searched it from top to bottom."

"Big deal. Just 'cause you didn't find it doesn't mean

it's not there. You're not foolproof, you know. I bet I could find it. Whatta you say, let's get on over there and give it a whirl."

"*I'll* get on over there. You go back up to bed."

"Like hell. It's my idea, I'm goin'. You go back up to bed."

"You're bleeding."

"Not anymore. And I won't, now I got my wooden leg back. Let's go."

They hurried as fast as Raider could over to the Macomber. They passed the narrow alley strewn with trash and were approaching the front door when Doc suddenly stopped.

"What's the matter?"

"Am I seeing things? Back up."

"Doc . . ."

Doc waved away objection, backtracked, and looked down the trash-filled alley and upward. A black leather case rose slowly.

"What the hell . . ." began Raider.

"Let's go!"

Doc outsprinted him easily, racing through the lobby and up the stairs to Utterby's room. Pausing before the door, he could hear Raider's crutch pounding up the stairs. He decided that if he could hear it, so could Utterby inside. He returned stealthily to the head of the stairs and, placing his finger against his lips, hissed, "Quiet. What happened to your rubber tip?"

"Musta fell off."

"Great, he can hear you coming for ten blocks. Set it down easily, softly."

"Oh bullshit, whatta ya gotta be so picky for?"

He came clomping and lumbering up the stairs. He started down the hall after Doc. Halfway to the door it burst open; Utterby leaned out and fired. But the noise of the door warned both men approaching. Doc ducked, and Raider flattened against the wall, his crutch tumbling to the floor, distracting Utterby just enough to affect his aim. The closest he came to either with his first four shots was one that narrowly missed ticking the tip of Raider's nose presented in profile. Before Utterby could get off a fifth shot Doc had his gun out and firing. Utterby's gun flew from his grasp.

"I'm hit!"

Doors flew open. People leaned out, their eyes rounding with fear.

"It's okay, folks," said Raider expansively. "Just a little friendly set-to. No great shakes. You can get back to your own business now if it's not too much trouble."

The two of them hurried the wounded Utterby back inside. Doc retrieved Elmo's gun.

"For such a great shot you're not much of a shot," said Raider.

"Over by the bed," ordered Doc.

"I should have killed you in the alley," growled Utterby to Raider.

"Oh shut up. Do you have to turn out a sore loser on top o' everythin' else? Where's the certificates?"

"In my makeup case. Well, gentlemen, it appears you have me. What now?"

"Whatta you think? You're goin' back to Frisco and stand trial, and I hope the judge gives you eighty years."

"Come now, let's not be nasty. Why don't we make a deal? There's more than a hundred thousand dollars worth of premium stock there, not to mention more than two thousand cash."

"Correction," said Doc dryly. "Your stock's worth more than a quarter of a million as of noon today."

"You don't say."

"I'm afraid we'll have to disappoint you, Elmo. No deals."

"I didn't think you'd go for it." His eyes went to Raider's. "You, brother, are a four-square ingrate. I saved your life. At the very least your leg."

"Bullshit. I coulda done a better job on myself. You'd best stick to figgerin' figgers and playactin'. You sure'll never be a doctor. You got the touch of a damn gorilla."

"We're leaving right away," said Doc. "Bring whatever you please with you, except your gun. We'll take good care of it."

"San Francisco. Oh well, it'll be a thrill to see the bay again."

"E.S. Hollenbeck will be thrilled to see you again. I think he'd appreciate the stock rather than the cash, what do you think?"

"I think you're rubbing salt in the wound."

"I think you deserve a little salt. There's one thing I'd appreciate your explaining. We've been back in town nearly forty minutes. You got here well ahead of us; what took you so long to get up here and retrieve your makeup case? How do you account for the delay?"

"I rode in and out again to the north. I got all the way to Red Lake before I changed my mind." He shrugged. "I decided to take a chance, come back, and get the case. Obviously I'm lost without it."

Raider smirked. "Brother, today's the day you're lost with it. Come on, Doc, let's get outta this dump and outta this town."

CHAPTER TWELVE

UTTERBY CAPTURED STOCK CERTIFICATES AND
REMAINING STOLEN CASH AMOUNTING TO 2014
CONFISCATED STOP RETURNING SF WITH PRIS-
ONER STOCK MONEY
OPW

Raider stood outside Western Union office waiting for
Doc to pay the clerk. Raider glared at the prisoner and spit.

"You don't much like me, do you, old boy?"

"Not much, old boy."

Doc came out. "All set, Rade."

"Why the chip on your shoulder, Rade?"

"Raider to you, old boy. It's simple: you're a wiseass;
you got no right toying with a man's 'motions."

"Mo . . . ?"

"He means *e*motions," explained Doc. "You'll get used
to his brutal interpretation of the language. If you think he's
bad you ought to hear Allan Pinkerton. *E*motions. I think

he's referring to your lady-in-red disguise."

Utterby laughed. Again Raider spat and glowered.

"I really enchanted you with that one, didn't I?"

"Horse's ass. You must be some kinda weirdo to waltz around dressed up like a woman."

"If that thought mitigates your embarrassment, by all means harbor it."

Raider bristled. "Wha'ja say? What'd he say?"

"Never mind," replied Doc. "Elmo, we'll ride to Williams and catch the Santa Fe Pacific. We'll switch over to the Atchison, Topeka, Santa Fe in Needles at the border. We'll change again to the Southern Pacific in Kerns. That'll take us home."

"You don't have to tell me, old boy. I know the Southern Pacific routes. Shall we go?"

The westbound train did not arrive in Williams until 9:22 in the evening. Doc went to make arrangements to ship their horses while Raider kept an eye on Utterby.

"You try anythin', 'old boy', and I'll put a hole in you the undertaker'll be able to hang his hat in."

"You don't have to threaten me, Raider, I know when I'm licked. I'm not exactly a hardened criminal, you know. Matter of fact, this is my first offense. I never stole a nickel before."

"Save it for the newspaper boys, why don'cha."

They stood on the station platform in the gathering darkness punctured by half a dozen dim lamps hanging from the roof and the feeble light inside the station.

"I could never be what they call a hardened criminal; I'm just not cut out for it. I could handle a gun, but I'd never be able to shoot anybody, not intentionally."

"It didn't bother you none to hire the Claggetts to, did it? They come after us hell bent for breakfast. Wha'ja do, offer a' extra bonus for them that potted us? That what you did?"

"You really dislike me."

"Whatta you care whether I like you or not? We're nothin' to each other."

"One doesn't altogether relish the idea of others disliking one."

"Oh, cut it out, you're not on the damn stage now. Nobody's gonna clap for you."

Doc came up. "The horses are all set. How are you two getting on? Not that well, if I read your faces rightly."

Raider grunted.

"A pity," said Utterby. "We've a long way to go. I was just saying I'm not your run-of-the-mill career criminal, Weatherbee."

"You did okay first time out," growled Raider.

"That's just it. First offense. Weatherbee, what do you think they'll do to me?"

"It's hard to say. It depends on the judge. If it's a jury trial, and under the law you have a right to one, I expect you could make points with them with a sob story." He stared at him appraisingly. "Why *did* you do it, Elmo?"

In response Utterby began his story. Sensing a long one, Raider turned about and trod heavily off out of hearing. Doc listened politely.

"What it comes down to is you couldn't take their thievery any longer."

"Not and help them steal, and cover up for them."

"Why didn't you just quit? Or did you feel you had to punish them?"

"Something like that."

"I don't see it as much of a punishment. Over a career as long as Hollenbeck's ninety-three thousand is a drop in the bucket. And, thanks to you, they'll be getting back three times the value."

"If that's the case, and I couldn't agree more, why should they bother to prosecute me? Frankly, I can hardly wait. Are they in for a surprise."

"Oh?"

"I don't intend to go down without a fight. Whatever

happens I'll end up in prison. When I stand up in the court-
room I'll give the world an earful, bet on it. Every yellow
rag in the country'll have a field day at the expense of
Southern Pacific. Hollenbeck and his gang won't be able
to show their faces in daylight. Don't be surprised if after
it's over he resigns. He and Cantor. They're the worst of-
fenders."

"You want vengeance."

"Wouldn't you?"

"What did either do to you, I mean personally? Did the
money they stole come out of your pocket?"

"It came out of Wilfred Trimble's, out of a lot of people's."

"Yours?"

"I suppose not directly, if you want to split hairs, old
boy, but that's not the point."

"What is?"

"They're thieves, every one of them. They've outstolen
me twentyfold. But they're not branded criminals, so they
won't go to prison. They get away with it and I'm made to
suffer. Is that fair?"

"No."

"You agree with me."

"No, he doesn't!" barked Raider. He started back toward
them. "You think their wrong makes what you did right?
That's what it sounds like you think. If you do it's bullshit.
You want fairness, go live on Mars or someplace. There's
no such thing in this world. You're a grown man, you gotta
brain in your head, you talk like you do, how come you
don't know there isn't? Whatta you been doin' all your life,
livin' in a damn bottle? You stole and you were caught and
you're gonna pay. All o' them'll pay, too, if not in this
world then the next. Whatever they did, whatever they're
doin', they gotta look in the mirror; they gotta look into
their old ladies' eyes, their kids', their friends', their preach-
ers', their own. You look down your nose at them. Hell!
You should pity 'em. Now shut up about it once and for

all. We're not innerested. Tell him, Doc."

Doc smiled benignly. "I guess we're not interested."

Raider and Doc shared the day watch over their prisoner and alternated the night, four hours on, four off. The trip by train was uneventful to the point of outright boredom, but in Raider's view "it beat by a High Plains mile the trip down on horseback in the rain nearly all the way." When they switched over to the Southern Pacific in Kern an arrestingly beautiful woman got on. Full-figured, statuesque, with the face of a *charmeuse*, according to Doc, she drew all eyes as she glided up the aisle and found a seat to her liking. In passing them she glanced at Raider. He made no comment, however. He had no wish to open the door to Utterby's sarcasm in recollection of the lady in red.

Doc felt no such constraint. "That, gentlemen, is enough to infuse my whole day with a golden glow," he whispered.

"Striking," said Utterby, and looked at Raider.

Raider grunted and looked out the window at the thickening vegetation as they approached Tulare Lake country. More than two hundred miles to the city by the bay stretched before them. Night was drawing on, the darkness cloaking the land. The train threaded through it with surprising swiftness. The whistle hooted, greeting it and dispatching a pair of enormous jackrabbits on a line at a perfect right angle to the train. Raider sat by the window, Utterby facing him opposite, Doc in the aisle seat next to his partner. Utterby was a portrait of relaxation, his head tilted back, neck resting on the top of the seat back, eyes languid, not a trace of tension in his expression. Had he been asleep he could not have looked more at ease.

Raider eyed him sourly. "You got no problem with your conscience, I see," he muttered.

"Would you prefer I did?"

"I couldn't care less one way or the other."

"Please don't start," cautioned Doc.

"Would you believe, the more I think about it, the more

eagerly I look forward to my day in court. I can't wait to get up and speak my piece and see Hollenbeck's face and the faces of the others."

On he prattled about his day in court and the "joyous prospect of heaping humiliation" on his former superiors. He was becoming fanatical on the subject. Raider's deepening scowl only encouraged him. Doc listened with half an ear. If the man was vengeance bent, and he was, it was his affair, his problem, actually. Doc didn't care a fig. Raider shouldn't let it bother him. At this stage it was all Utterby had left.

It could also serve another purpose—to distract them both, make them think he was so eager to speak out in court that wild horses couldn't keep him from getting there. That escape was the last thought in his mind. In both Needles and Kern in changing trains he had behaved like a model prisoner en route. There were eight stops between here and San Francisco, beginning with Tipton in addition to the changeover from the northbound to the west-and-north-bound S.P. line in Visalia, but, resolved Doc, looking askance at Utterby, who continued to regale them with talk of his revenge, they wouldn't allow him to get off for any reason. He probably wouldn't ask to. If he had to go to the bathroom there was the necessary at the front end of the car; if he wanted to stretch his legs he could use the aisle; if he was hungry, if he wanted a newspaper, if he wanted anything within reason, one or the other could get off and procure it for him.

Doc's instincts advised that if Utterby were thinking of making a break for it he'd most likely wait until their destination. He'd lived in San Francisco for years, knew the city, knew where he could flee to and hide safely. And he had friends there whom he could count on to help him.

They would take him off the train, march him through Union Station to a hansom to the California Street jail. Deliver him, get him out of their hands. From the jail they would go to the Southern Pacific office and report to E. S.

Hollenbeck. They'd return the $2,014, hand over the stock certificates, and get receipts for both. That, hopefully, would be the end of it. There was of course the possibility that they'd be required to testify at his trial. A written statement generally sufficed, but occasionally they were asked to be present.

"Hollenbeck professes to be deeply religious," said Utterby. "Church deacon, reads his Bible even in the office, liberal doner to his church over and above tithing, typical pillar of the community. If his friends and neighbors ever knew the truth, if his family did . . . and they will."

"You'll see to it," muttered Raider. "Tell me somethin', old boy."

"Anything."

"Do me a favor and think about it before you answer. Be honest, did you hate him as much before you were caught as you do now? Or did gettin' caught light a fire under your hate?"

"I've hated him from the beginning. Nothing could happen, there's nothing he could do that could possibly increase my loathing of the man. Is it possible to make poison more poisonous?"

"You're a goddamn liar! You're sore as hell 'cause you were caught; your pride hurts like hell, and so does your dumb vanity, so you take it out on him. You're as phony as a thimble-rigger working a charity for widows and orphans."

"You're a stupid man, Raider."

"Ahhhh, hear that, Doc? I struck a nerve."

"Illiterate mongrel."

"Cut it out, Elmo," said Doc. "You, too, Rade. Why don't you two take a snooze? We're due in at seven-thirty in the morning, thanks to the switchover in Visalia to the coast run and layovers in Salinas, Santa Cruz, and San Mateo. Go to sleep, both of you. I'll wake you in four hours, Rade."

Raider grunted, stretched, slumped, tilted his hat down

over his face, and in ten seconds was snoring lustily.

"Illiterate mongrel," repeated Utterby.

"You say that once more and I'll break your face," said Doc mildly.

Utterby stared. "You mean it."

"Please say it."

It was announced that the train would be making a two-minute unscheduled stop in Belmont, a sleepy little town nestled at the bottom of virtually treeless hills and only a few minutes out of San Francisco. The announcement woke Doc. His watch read 7:15. Raider had relieved him at 4:00 A.M. Utterby was awake. Doc blinked the sleep from his eyes, ran his sour-tasting tongue around inside his mouth, stifled a yawn, and stretched.

"I have to go to the bathroom," said Utterby.

Doc glanced at Raider. "I'll go."

"I will. You went the last two times. I need to stretch my leg."

Doc watched his partner thump loudly up the aisle, waking passengers left and right, Utterby preceding him, executing arm exercises as he approached the necessary. He went inside. Raider passed through the end door into the vestibule.

He leaned out the open window; the wind slammed against his face. It felt invigorating. Overhead soot-studded smoke escaped the diamond stack and plumed back down the string of cars. He glanced to his left; Utterby was making no attempt to climb out the window. One of them had to accompany him when nature called just to make sure he didn't try anything rash or clever. Raider had him pegged; he didn't believe for a moment he'd meekly accompany them to the California Street jail when they got in. But he didn't think he'd try anything on the train. Instead, when they got off he'd ask to go to the bathroom again; they'd go with him. He'd protest when one or the other accompanied him inside. In vain.

He knew that he'd be the one Utterby would work on. It wasn't two men against one, it was three legs against two, and his crutch made it all but impossible for him to pursue should "old boy" try and make a break for it.

Before they got off he'd give his bandanna to Doc to wrap around his hand to conceal his .38 in it. They'd march Utterby through the crowd to the curb outside with the gun pressed against his kidney. Escorted so, he wouldn't dare miss a step much less try and get away.

He pulled in his head and sucked his lungs full. He was famished. He could eat two T-bone steaks and a plateful of fried potatoes. A pot of coffee would wash them down nicely. He turned to look through the end door window and up the aisle. Passengers dozed. A few were preparing to get off. The conductor had stopped to talk to Doc. Turning back to the vestibule window, he leaned out a second time. Utterby was leaning out his window.

"Invigorating, isn't it?"

Raider grunted.

The conductor took off his cap and ran his handkerchief around the lining.

"Going to be another scorcher." He smiled, showing a single gleaming gold tooth in line with a host of yellowed ones. Perspiration had wilted his collar, and his jacket looked to be wringing wet. "What can I do for you?"

"My partner and I have horses in the next-to-last car. Can they be taken off for us at the station and held for a couple of hours? We've some things to do that require our immediate attention."

"There's a pen at the north end of the station. Cost you a buck apiece. You got your receipt stubs?"

Doc gave him the stubs and two dollars.

"They can only hold them till sundown, and it's extra if they have to feed them. Water's free."

"Somebody will be picking them up before noon."

"I'll see to it."

"I appreciate it."

"You didn't happen to see who got on in Visalia, did you?"

Doc shook his head.

"Five women, W.C.T.U.ers—you know, Christian Temperance. Some bigwig by the name of Carry Nation, her and four other booze busters. She's on her way to San Francisco to lecture. Ever hear of her?"

"No."

"I understand she's some great shakes back in Kansas. Dead against drink. You know those temperance types. She's six foot tall if she's an inch, built like a brickyard, with a face like a bull terrior. You'll see her when you get off. I'll see to your horses."

Raider and Utterby came back. Belmont arrived and two minutes later began slipping behind. The engineer let loose a single long blast announcing their imminent arrival at Union Station.

Utterby started off behind Raider without even glancing upward at his bag and makeup case in the overhead rack.

"Aren't you forgetting something?" asked Doc behind him. He had wrapped his gun in his right hand with Raider's bandanna.

"Of course," responded Utterby. "How forgetful of me."

Raider sniffed and accorded him a look that condemned his intelligence.

"I'll be right behind you every step," cautioned Doc. "If you try anything at all I'll be forced to act, so think twice."

"You'll shoot me, kill me in cold blood in a crowded station. Of course. Who do you think you're kidding?"

"I'll be so close I won't hit anybody but you."

"Don't tempt him," said Raider. "Man's got the itchiest trigger finger in the whole agency."

Utterby snickered.

They started up the aisle. The platform was mobbed with women. All wore golden sashes with W.C.T.U. inscribed

in stark black letters. Many carried signs; some wore sand-
wich posters; one was dressed in a cloth bottle, her face
surrounded by the neck and the label reading:

DRINK ME
XXX
I'M 100 PROOF POISON

The signs were equally critical of drink and drunkenness:

"WHISKEY, THE NECTAR OF THE GODLESS!"
"DELIVER US FROM THE EVIL OF DEMON RUM!"
"BOOZERS ARE LOSERS"
"IGNOBLE DRINK, THE BANE OF MAN"
"SIGN THE PLEDGE"
"CRAWL FROM THE SLIMY OOZE, YE DROWNED DRUN-
KARDS, AND SPEAK OUT AGAINST DRINK!"

"Lips that Touch Liquor Will Never Touch Mine" was
displayed under a strikingly homely face. A loud, sustained
cheer and spirited applause went up, directed at a stout
woman in a black alpaca dress and bonnet crowning a face
so fierce "It'd scare a hungry dog outta a butcher shop," as
Raider observed.

They got off and, led by Raider, started to circle the
crowd to pass behind it and gain the ramp leading into the
station proper. The cheering grew louder. Mrs. Nation stood
on the first step of the car, waving to her well-wishers and
idolizers and blowing kisses while her escorts took up their
positions in a protective line in front of her. Aided by the
step and her own imposing height, she towered over them.
Women began to throw roses, and the crowd surged forward,
threatening to smother her with adulation. The two Pinkertons and their prisoner were almost in the clear when a
shout went up. At the head of the ramp which they'd started
up appeared a horde of men in shirtsleeves and aprons,
carrying signs of their own:

"GIVE STRONG DRINK UNTO HIM THAT IS READY TO PER-
ISH, AND WINE UNTO THOSE THAT BE OF HEAVY HEART.
LET HIM DRINK AND FORGET HIS POVERTY AND REMEM-
BER HIS MISERY NO MORE."

PROV. XXXI. 6.7.

"DRINK, YEA, DRINK ABUNDANTLY,
O BELOVED."

SONG OF SOLOMON V. 1ST.

"THE SON OF MAN CAME EATING AND DRINKING"

MATTHEW XI. 19.

"WINE WHICH CHEERETH GOD AND
MAN"

JUD. IX. 13.

"DRINK THY WINE WITH A MERRY
HEART"

ECCL. IX. 7.

Along with signs the new arrivals also carried brickbats
and baseball bats.

"Good Lord," rasped Doc.

They stood squarely in the path of the onrushing advo-
cates of strong drink. As one they turned. The women on
the platform had caught sight of the enemy. They started
up the ramp to meet them, yelling defiantly, wielding their
signs, umbrellas, parasols, and reticules well weighted with
bricks. Raider swore, grabbing the railing with one hand,
and raised his crutch to defend himself against the men.
Then swung around to do the same against the women,
forcing Doc to duck to avoid being clobbered. Utterby seized
his chance. Clapping one hand on the railing, he vaulted
over it, dropped three feet to the platform below, and, find-

ing himself in the clear, sprinted off. Raider yelled, and
Doc was about to follow when the tidal wave of womanhood
struck from behind. In a split second both operatives found
themselves sandwiched between the two armies. Screaming,
bellowing, brickbats and baseball bats waved threateningly,
anti-liquor signs crashing down on unprotected heads, including Doc's, and a surging, ear-splitting, bone-crushing
free-for-all. The bartenders appeared determined to get at
Carry Nation; the temperance ladies were just as determined
to prevent it. Neither side seemed to notice the two non-
combatants trapped between.

Doc turned and pushed with all his strength, trying to
force his way back down the ramp, yelling to Raider to get
behind him. It was less than two yards back to the platform
and around it out of the fray, but it speedily became twice
that when a lady twice the size of anyone near her, woman
or man, set her bulk squarely in Doc's way. He couldn't
get through her, couldn't get around her either side.

"Please, please, let us through."

"Sot! Wretch! Hyena! Shameless pervert! Glory to God,
peace on earth, and good will to all sober men! And all
drunken fiddlers, soaks and sponges, bloaters, blotters and
boozers, take your bottles and stagger to hell! One nation
indivisible! Carry Nation for all! Take that!"

Down came her umbrella, slamming him on the pate.
He shook off the blow, ducked under her upraised arm, and,
hauling Raider behind him by a fistful of shirt, got both of
them behind her and between two slender, screaming union-
ists off the ramp and back onto the platform.

It wasn't until they were in the clear that he discovered
that Raider had lost his crutch. They spotted it partway up
the ramp in the hands of Doc's overweight assailant, pressed
into service jamming bartenders in their throats with the
armrest, snapping their heads back sharply.

"My crutch, my crutch! Doc!"

"Forget it, Rade, I wouldn't go back in there with a suit
of armor and a Gatling gun!"

CHAPTER THIRTEEN

Everett Scott Hollenbeck's office was luxuriously furnished
in mahogany, teak, and other exotic woods, pungent leath-
ers, and regal-looking drapes. The floor was almost completely covered by a magnificent Persian carpet. His desk
was large enough to seat five people on one side. Portraits
of U.S. Presidents, other original paintings, and assorted
photographs of railroad tycoons graced the walls, but the
visitor's attention was immediately drawn to an enormous
rectangular fish tank filled with tropical fish of many colors
occupying the windowsill behind Hollenbeck's high-back
leather posture chair.

The Southern Pacific's president was a large man flirting
with corpulence, florid faced, stern-eyed, whose expres-
sions were pretty much restricted to three: a patronizing
smile, a no-nonsense frown, and a faraway look that suggested his mind was wandering from his visitor's words.
When Raider and Doc entered he was standing at the window, feeding his fish. Recognizing Doc, he greeted him
effusively.

"I got a telegram from your Mr. Wagner in Chicago not ten minutes ago telling me the good news. So you finally caught up with the dreadful cad, the devious, ungrateful scoundrel." He rubbed his hands briskly. "Sit, sit, sit. What have you done with him? Packed him off to jail, I imagine. Hee hee hee. You certainly wouldn't drag him around town with a rope around his neck, exhibiting him like a trained ape, though it would serve him right. Behind bars is where he belongs and where he'll stay."

"Sir . . ." began Doc.

"I have to be frank, Lissenbee. When I first got wind of this mess I was crushed. It was a staggering blow. This company and I personally had always treated him like a prince. Gave him everything he asked for, including his predecessor's job, and don't you think there are twenty men in that department who'd give their eyeteeth, even their right arms to be chief paymaster? To think he'd turn on us like that, to think he'd be so treacherous, so unappreciative. I treated him like I would my own son."

"Sir . . ."

"If there's one flaw I cannot bring myself to abide over all others it's dishonesty. It's a cardinal sin, the destruction of many a man. I'll be blunt, hanging is too good for the man who deserts the path of honesty. I'll tell you a little secret that musn't go beyond these walls. The day I heard, instead of going to lunch, I went to church. I prayed, gentlemen, to a kind and forgiving God to show him the error of his ways. Make him see what he'd done to me, to himself. I prayed that night, too. If he'd come straight back, I would have welcomed him with open arms and forgiven him on the spot."

"Sir . . ."

"The real pity is he didn't have to steal; if he needed money all he had to do was come to me. I wouldn't dream of turning him away empty-handed, or any other employee who finds himself temporarily up against it. We're all one big happy family here. I guess you could call me the daddy. I suppose I should go over to the jail and see him, give him the chance to ask my forgiveness. That's the Christian way. You know what the Bible says: knowledge puffeth up, but charity edifieth. Only I can't see him face to face, not right away. Don't misunderstand, criminals don't terrify me, but I can't help feeling uncomfortable in their presence. I do wish he'd write me a letter acknowledging his crime, asking for forgiveness. I'd read it. Next time you see him tell him so.

"Now then, you've brought the money back..."

"Sir..."

"You haven't? But in your telegram to your superiors—"

"Mr. Hollenbeck, what he's tryin' to tell you is Utterby got away."

"He certainly couldn't have spent it all in such a short time. Oh dear me, I'm forgetting; how careless of me; you mentioned that he'd brought stock. Wagner said a silver mine."

"This boy's deaf as a post," said Raider.

"Mr. Hollenbeck, we have the stock, we have over two thousand in cash. The stock has appreciated since he bought it; as of two days ago it was worth over a hundred thousand dollars. The company's actually coming out ahead."

"Did I hear you correctly?"

"We're both of us tryin' to tell you he got away. In the Union Station. Wasn't our fault. Doc had him covered tighter than a baby frog's asshole. We got san'wiched between a buncha barkeepers and a whole crowd o' wild women."

Hollenbeck's expression was suddenly that of a man who had accidentally shot himself. Astonishment stretched his face in every direction and thrust his eyeballs so far forward they threatened to drop free.

"Got away?"

"You shoulda been there. It was a combination o' the Little Bighorn, the burnin' of Atlanta, and a damn bank panic. There's prob'ly sixteen people killed and a hundred and sixteen hurt. We were lucky as hell to get outta there alive. I even lost my crutch. He got away."

"He's still in town," said Doc, licking his lips nervously. "He can't go anywhere without money, and we got every cent he had on him."

"You can't say that, Doc. We got better'n two thousand, sure, but there was three thousand left after he bought into the Belinda. He give some to the Claggetts to go after us, but sometime after we collared and searched him he coulda sneaked a couple hundred into his shoe. Coulda before we caught up with him. You didn't search his shoes, didja?"

"Did you?"

Hollenbeck found his voice. "You incompetent simpletons! Blundering idiots!"

"Hey, hey, hey," cautioned Raider. "There's no need to start name-callin'. It wasn't our fault he got away." He flexed his injured leg and winced. Walking without his crutch had been painful.

"You carry guns!" snapped Hollenbeck. "Why didn't you shoot him? He deserves to be shot! Nobody deserves it more!"

"Please," purred Doc. "Just listen. He's our responsibility. We caught him once; we'll catch him again. I give you my solemn word, neither of us will rest until we do. In the meantime..." He got out two envelopes, one twice the size of the other. "Here's the cash, two thousand and fourteen dollars. And the stock certificates. He bought eighteen hundred shares at fifty dollars a share. As of two days ago, as I said, they'd risen to fifty-six dollars, netting him ten thousand eight hundred paper profit. The Belinda is proving a genuine bonanza. The stock will double in no time. You might want to check it in today's paper. If it hasn't broken sixty, it'll be close to it."

Hollenbeck grunted. "That's reassuring, but it doesn't change things—I'm talking about him. You two botched it completely. Your chief recommended you as the best men for the job. I don't want to be rude, but if you two are the best the Pinkertons have to offer, I'd hate to see the worst."

"Go to hell," rasped Raider.

Hollenbeck started. Fury filled his face.

"Take it easy, Rade. Mr. Hollenbeck, we did blunder, no question, but you do have the money back, and, as I say, we'll get him. I apologize for our having lost him."

"That makes my whole day," he said sneeringly.

Raider struggled to his feet. "Let's get outta here, Doc." The door opened. Raider sat back down.

"J.B.," said Hollenbeck to the newcomer.

The man was so tall he had to stoop to avoid hitting his forehead on the top of the door frame. He looked like a ghost in an expensive cashmere suit. His fingernails were too long, aftershave powder rendered his cheeks pasty-looking, whatever blood his body contained appeared to have collected in his liver or kidneys or some other organ, depriving the rest of him of normal circulation and the glow of good health. Under his arm was a newspaper. Hollenbeck curtly introduced Vice-President J. B. Cantor.

"Did you see this morning's paper, Ev?"

"Not yet."

"There's a piece about that silver mine."

"The Belinda?" asked Raider.

Cantor ignored him, keeping his rheumy eyes fastened on Hollenbeck. "Didn't that fellow Wagner or whatever his name is with the detective agency mention his office had gotten a report that Utterby had invested the money in mining stocks?"

"Here they are," said Hollenbeck, holding them up and fanning them like a poker hand.

"May I?"

Cantor took one from him and studied it. He rubbed his thumb over the face of it. Then without a word he strode to the fish tank and immersed the certificate.

"What the hell..." began Hollenbeck.

"Look, look." Cantor returned the dripping certificate to the desk.

"Holy jumpin'..." began Raider.

"Good Lord," murmured Doc.

Hollenbeck gasped. The water had smeared the rose-colored printing and emblem into indistinguishability.

"Let me see that," said Doc, snatching it from Cantor.

"It's a phony," said Cantor. "Probably not worth the paper it's printed on."

Hollenbeck sat still as stone, breathing noisily through his nose, gaping straight ahead, utterly, completely dumbfounded.

"Listen to this," said Cantor. He unfolded the newspaper and quickly found the item. "Here we are. 'Eustace Atherton, president of the Majority Miners and Merchants Bank, licensed distributor of both common and preferred stock in the Big Bonanza Company Limited, parent company of the Belinda diggings, was last seen leaving the bank at closing time two days ago. He did not come to work the next morning and has not been seen since. Vice-President Orus Talmadge conducted a detailed examination of the Bonanza stock account under the watchful eye of Marshal Evan Rhilander. It was discovered that Atherton or a confederate had secretly printed counterfeit stock certificates. These were sold to investors; Atherton then used the money to buy legitimate stock. He kept a strict accounting, and after the bank's handling fees were deducted the remaining funds were turned over to the mine owners to pay for day-to-day operations and new explorations. Complete figures are not yet available and may not be for some time. Talmadge and others, however, estimate that less than twenty percent of the legitimate certificates were distributed to investors. The remaining more than eighty percent was stolen by Atherton.' Do you want to hear more?"

Hollenbeck came out of his paralysis. He waved his hand, dismissing any further reading.

"How about that!" exclaimed Raider, then furrowed his brow. "But I don't get it. I mean, I understand how he used folk's money to buy the real stock, but then he handed the money they gave him over to the mine."

"He had to," said Doc. "The stock was selling like crazy.

He couldn't bury the money in the ground. He wasn't interested in the money. What he wanted was the lion's share
of the stock, and he's got it."

"Better than eighty percent," said Cantor.

"What the hell good does it do him?" asked Raider, still
confused.

"Are you kidding? It'll start paying dividends; he can
hang on to some, cash in the rest when it peaks." Doc shook
his head admiringly. "He's sitting on top of the world."

"How can you say that? He can't even show his face.
He's gotta either keep runnin' or hide out the next twenty
years, maybe the rest of his life. He can't collect a dime."

"Oh yes he can," said Cantor. "He can hire people to act
as his agents. The Big Bonanza Company doesn't care. They
got their money. They're perfectly willing to pay dividends,
authorize changes in control of blocs of shares. He can cash
in every share he's pilferred for whatever the value may be
at the time, and never show his face, never betray his where-
abouts, and never risk getting caught. Believe me, it's been
done before."

"This stock's worthless," said Hollenbeck hoarsely. He
began growling deep in his throat, and his face took on a
fearsome aspect.

The three of them stared at him.

"This is all Utterby's doing."

"No, no, no," said Cantor. "It's this Atherton, the bank
president."

"Utterby! I'll get him and get even if it's the last thing
I do on this earth. So help me I will."

"Ev..."

"I'll strangle him! Oh, how I'd love to get his neck in
these hands ... I'll rip him limb from limb! I'll crush him
to death! His screams'll be music to my ears! You hear me?
You hear? Utterrrrrrrbyyyyyyy, wherever you are I'll get
you! You're a dead man, Utterrrrrrrrbyyyyyy!"

The door flew wide. Three secretaries stared fearfully.
Two men came up behind them gawking. Hollenbeck was

raving, ranting, coming out from behind his desk, storming about, smashing the air with his fists, his face purpling, the veins in his neck roping. He was suddenly a man deliberately courting a heart attack. A man gone wild!

Raider got up and backed limping away from him. Doc followed, backing the two of them out.

Downstairs they emerged from the elevator. Doc helped Raidor to the door and out onto the sidewalk. Doc hadn't uttered a sound since leaving the office, so stunned was he by Cantor's disclosure. So shocked he couldn't find words.

Raider had no such difficulty. "Old A.P. gets wind o' this we'll be in for it in spades, Weatherbee, watch and see."

"Mmmmm."

"He'll send us packin' right back out again lookin' for Mr. Candy Atherton and Elmo. Whatta ya say, how's about we flip a coin, see who goes after the old boy?"

"Rade..." Doc stood studying Raider with a soulful expression, the look of a well-whipped hound. "Don't talk. There's nothing you can say that means anything. Let's just go get breakfast. Let's get a drink. Let's get you a new crutch. Let's get the horses. Let's—"

"What?"

"The man is stark, staring loony. He is. He's liable to get a gun and go after Elmo himself."

"Forget him, Doc. What are we gonna do?"

"There isn't much we can do but sit tight and wait for orders."

"Old boy Elmo'll get away for sure."

"Hasn't he already? Oh Lord, wait till the chief gets wind of this. Just wait."

CHAPTER FOURTEEN

They took a room at the Palace Hotel, a great, sprawling building eight stories high that had reputedly cost a million dollars a floor to build and furnish. Marble statues abounded; in the lobby was a fountain as large as the Trevi fountain in Rome; miles of imported carpeting swathed floors of oak fashioned from trees grown on a ranch owned by banker William C. Ralston, the builder.

It was Doc's contention that if he and Raider had to go down they might as well go in style. Raider agreed. They sat in one of the hotel's four sumptuous dining rooms under a thousand pounds of crystal chandelier, surrounded by opulence and beauty, enjoying a leisurely supper, both men battling the urge to brood over the debacle that the Elmo Utterby case had become. Raider was in a rare expansive mood. They shared a bottle of white wine, and it seemed to mellow the plowboy, relaxing him, dispelling his characteristic annoyance, and imbuing him with tolerance.

"I don't have to tell you Utterby rubbed me the wrong

132

way from day one, Doc, but now thinkin' back on him he wasn't such a bad sort. A wiseass, maybe, and highfalutin' for a nothin' pencil-pushin' figger filbert, but ace-high straight compared to that purple-faced son-of-a-bitchin' Hollenbeck. Chrissakes, the way he carried on you'd think the ninety-three thousand come out his pocket."

Doc snickered. "It did. It represents money Utterby didn't give him a chance to get around to stealing."

"You're right. Hey, what's this stuff we're drinkin'?"

"A commendable white Graves—a Bordeaux wine."

"Got no kick, but it tastes nice."

Two young women were approaching. Up to the table they marched, both smiling graciously and proferring leaflets advertising Mrs. Carry A. Nation's speech at a local theater. The taller of the two, a pretty redhead, stared disdainfully at the bottle set between Raider and Doc. Doc politely accepted and read the leaflet. Raider started to, saw what it was, crumpled it, and handed it back. The lady who'd given it to him looked as if he'd just strangled her firstborn.

"Not innerested, thanks."

"Rade..."

"You ladies like a drink?"

"Rade!"

The redhead sniffed, elevated her nose, and glared. Her companion looked distressed to the point of outright shock. Off they sailed.

"You didn't have to be rude."

"Wasn't they? Innerruptin' us 'thout so much as 'scuse me. If you ask me they oughta put that scow barge Carry A. Nation in a box and ship her back to Kansas. I mean if she doesn't like liquor she doesn't have to, but she shouldn't be goin' around tellin' others not to drink, and causin' riots and such."

Doc sensed a long lecture forthcoming. To his relief a bellboy in brass buttons and pillbox cap approached, carrying a salver with a familiar-looking yellow envelope on

it. The telegram's arrival did inspire relief, until Doc began
to speculate on the contents. A small chill chased up his
spine. He snatched up the envelope and tore it open. "Tip
the man, Rade."

"Me?"

"Give him a tip."

The bellboy stood poker straight, staring through Raider,
his tray under his arm. Raider dug, came up with a quarter,
was about to hand it to him, changed his mind, put it back
in his pocket, and gave him a nickel.

"Who's it from, A.P.?

"William."

"Oh for Chrissakes!"

"Sssssh. He's in Los Angeles. Hollenbeck or somebody
with the Southern Pacific must have contacted Bill Wagner
with the good news. Evidently the chief hasn't gotten back
to Chicago yet. Wagner wired William in L.A. He says we're
to stay here until he arrives. He's on his way."

"Great! That's all we need, Mr. Big Eye Walrus Mustache
buttin' in. Watch, he'll come up with some harebrained
scheme that makes no sense at all."

"Relax, better him than his father."

"We don't need neither."

"He'll be in at eight-ten tonight." Doc checked his pocket
watch. "It's five after six. That gives us two hours."

"To do what?"

"Come up with a workable plan to pick up the threads
of this thing. All we've done for the past two days is talk,
talk, talk. We haven't formulated anything worthwhile."

"I already told you the plan: forget about Utterby, go
after Candy Atherton. The whole idea's to get back the
money; so we can't, so the next best thing's the stock, the
real stock. Utterby hasn't got it; Atherton has. We go back
to Mortality and start lookin' for him."

"Everybody in town is looking for him."

"Does that mean we shouldn't? Hey, hey, hey, hey."
Raider's face brightened, he moved forward in his chair.

"Wait, wait, wait. Utterby..."

"What about him?"

"Wherever he's got to, whatever he's doin', he's readin' the papers, he knows what's goin' on."

Doc agreed. "Yes, he must know what Atherton's done. He'll be going after him too. We could end up catching them together."

"A.P.'d like that. Whatta you say, let's make believe we didn't get any telegram from William and take off right now. Whatta you say, Doc?"

"Please, let's not get any deeper in dutch then we already are. I'm going to have the raspberry sherbert with the marshmallow fluff for dessert, how about you?"

"I'm gonna have whiskey." He raised his wine glass. "Here's to ya, Mrs. Nation."

William Pinkerton bore not the slightest resemblance to his famous father, or his mother for that matter. He was not a handsome man. He wore his light brown hair plastered across his head and displayed a mustache that approached walrus size under his prominent nose. Failure to confine his mustache to the area bounded by the corners of his mouth was a mistake. Nature had given him a walrus-like appearance: what with large, protruding eyes and a keglike head joining his chest with no visible presence of a neck, the addition of the oversized mustache only emphasized his similarity to a walrus. He was Allan Pinkerton's eldest son— a decent sort, not at all temperamental like his father; he was fair, not in the least overbearing; he wielded the carrot of authority rather than the stick. But he was not as shrewd or as experienced as the chief, and his thinking was frequently muddled, in particular when he came into a case late, as he did now. The three sat in one of the Palace Hotel's five bars in a booth in a council of war.

William sipped his ale and looked about. "You boys enjoy living high on the hog at the agency's expense?" he asked good-naturedly.

"This here's the only place we could get a room," replied Raider. "Every other hotel in town is filled to busting, even the fleabags down by the dock. There's a' anti-saloon Christian Temperance convention in town. It's overrun with women with signs and leaflets and such."

William grinned. "I see." He winked at Doc and glanced down the eighty-foot bar, its surface shining like glass under six chandeliers. A lone drinker footed the brass rail. At his disposal were six bartenders.

"I don't know all the angles on this case, obviously, but from what I've been able to get out of Bill Wagner and the newspaper stories this bank president is the one we should concentrate on."

"Agreed," said Doc.

"We've simply got to catch him. E. S. Hollenbeck is up in arms. He's threatening to break the line's contract with the agency, sue us, and sue my father personally for botching the thing."

Raider flared indignantly. "We didn't botch nothing! Utterby got away, but he's small fry. Atherton's the big fish, and we didn't have any way o' knowin' that till the story broke in the *Chronicle*. If we botched Atherton, everybody in Mortality did too. He suckered them all."

"Everybody in Mortality isn't working for the Southern Pacific. I'm not critizing you, Raider. If anything you have my sympathy. But I can't overemphasize the seriousness of our position. If we fail to catch up with Atherton and recover the legitimate certificates, at least the Southern Pacific's portion, Hollenbeck will cancel the contract, and other railroads may think twice about hiring us. Lines we already have contracts with may break them. Hollenbeck may encourage them to. He's a vindictive man."

"You don't have to tell us," said Raider. "We've seen him in action. He's loco."

"We've got to find Atherton."

"I don't want to be pessimistic," said Doc, "but it's not going to be easy. He's got plenty of money and the whole world to hide in. He can run off to Bulgaria and sit on that stock for the next ten years."

"Be that as it may, we've got to try. First thing in the morning we're heading out for Mortality."

Both nodded. William talked on, citing another case both were familiar with in comparison. Doc only half listened. To say their work was cut out for them, he mused ruefully, would be putting it so mildly it didn't warrant mentioning. Atherton had planned very well. He'd carried on his nefarious scheme until satisfied that continuing to do so threatened danger, whereupon he'd packed his stock and his shirts and left town. Wherever he lit, in Texas or Tahiti, he'd arrive flush and sitting pretty, able to hire an army to protect him. He could certainly afford a lot better than the Claggetts, Utterby's protection choice of necessity.

Once they got back to Mortality they would have to talk to everyone who knew Atherton well, people like his vice-president, everyone in the bank, the marshal. With luck they might be able to establish some sort of pattern to the banker's life, a style, that given the wherewithal and the freedom might be a clue to where he'd gone. There might be one place he'd dreamt of going to all his life. To be sure, if he talked about it, if people knew, it would be the last place he'd head for. Still, it was an angle that shouldn't be overlooked.

For all its foreboding aspects, and they seemed endless, the case did have its amusing side. They had spent all those hours chasing around after Utterby, finally catching him and bringing him back—only to lose him—arriving in Hollenbeck's office to discover that Atherton was the real culprit all along. How he must be laughing at them right now, knowing how hard they'd worked to track down Utterby.

Most criminals when unmasked didn't surprise Doc; Atherton did. If ever there was a prototype of the banker breed, the candy lover was it. He played the part to a tee. Outwardly, an absolute paragon of rectitude. Not that bankers weren't venal and some villainous, but he just didn't *seem* the type. Didn't look as if he had the necessary spleen; did look as if he reveled in the respect and recognition his position gave him. Such a friendly sort, always smiling, no black moods or temperamental outbursts, the soul of politeness and cooperation.

Utterby. He was amazingly resourceful. After all he'd gone through, to lose out to Atherton in the end must gall him tremendously. He must be furious! Raider was right— he'd be out looking for him. And if and when he caught up with him, he might be angry enough to shoot him, despite his professed incapacity for violence.

CHAPTER FIFTEEN

William Pinkerton elected to travel by train. To simplify the journey Raider and Doc would leave their horses in San Francisco and rent others upon arriving. Five minutes before their train came in, who should come stomping up but E. S. Hollenbeck. He looked a wreck—his clothes were rumpled, his hair in disarray, he was unshaven, his eyes were crimson from lack of sleep. He looked as if the tantrum he had thrown in his office three days earlier had persisted without letup. He was furious. He ignored Raider and Doc and confronted William, standing so close as he launched his harangue that their vest buttons touched.

"Pinkerton . . ."

"William," said William, backing away a step and smiling.

"I've sent a dozen wires off to your father. Told him the whole sorry story. Told him too this is your last chance. You're to find Utterby and that other scoundrel, the banker, and bring them back in chains if need be. Back to my office.

I mean before you turn them over to the police, to anybody. Is that clear? That's an order."

"I'm afraid we can't do that, Mr. Hollenbeck. We—"

"You'll do as you're damn well told, impertinent pup!"

"I don't think you understand."

They were attracting a crowd. William's eyes darted left and right as he noticed. Hollenbeck ignored the rubberneckers.

"It's you who don't understand!"

"If you'll let me explain . . . As a matter of agency policy, when we apprehend suspects we have to turn them over to the nearest authorized law enforcement agency. In this instance they'll be brought back here—at least Utterby will—and turned over to the police."

"You dare defy me! You'll bring them both back to me or I'll destroy you and your old man and his precious agency! I've already apprised our lawyers of this miserable affair and—he turned to Raider, then Doc—"your incompetence in conducting your investigation, your utter and complete failure to fulfill your end of the contract. Before I'm done I'm going to personally make the Pinkerton National Detective Agency the laughingstock of the country. You deserve to be pilloried, and that's what you'll get. Before I'm done the public'll be ridiculing you and throwing tomatoes at you. You'll be the object of scorn and derision in every state in the Union. I intend to sue you down from your high horses straight into the poorhouse.

"There's only one way you can prevent it, and you know what it is. Now you get on that train and get over there and do what you have to. I'm giving you one week!"

"I'm giving you some words of advice," said William mildly. "You go to hell."

The crowd oohed and ahhed. Doc stiffened. Raider grinned so swiftly and so expansively he nearly cracked his face. Hollenbeck froze. His eyes bulged, his lower lip quivered, color rose darkening to his eyebrows, his veins protruded, his rage accumulated, his hands shook. But he did not respond. Instead, he turned on his heel and marched off, elbowing aside first one, then another bystander who happened to be in his way. All eyes turned from him back to William.

Raider applauded. "That's tellin' him, Billy!"

"I shouldn't have said that. Dad'll flay me alive. But you know something?" He paused, beamed warmly, and sucked air in over his mustache. "It's worth it."

"The man *is* a little bit loony," observed Doc.

"Cross your fingers, boys," said Raider. "Maybe we'll get lucky. Maybe he'll go back to his office and put a bullet through his head."

A bell sounded far down the track, the whistle sang, and—whooshing, clanking, rattling, groaning, and chuffing—the train arrived. Preoccupied with discussing Hollenbeck with William, Raider and Doc failed to see the middle-aged, clean-shaven man carrying a leather case and the suitcase they'd last seen going over the side of the ramp board the train.

He saw them.

Mortality was as rife with frustration and fury as Doc predicted it would be. Nearly everyone in town had bought at least two shares in the Big Bonanza Company. One out of five shares was genuine. The earliest investors were the lucky ones. The differences between the genuine and the counterfeit were not easy to distinguish with the naked eye even when they were placed side by side under a strong light. Marshal Rhilander pointed this out to Raider, Doc, and William in his office. Virgil and Elon Claggett still languished in their cells, waiting for the circuit judge to arrive and try them.

"I bought five shares two hours after the strike was announced," said the marshal. "I bought five more three days later. This is one of the first five; this, one of the second. As you can see, the rose color is identical, and the scrollwork too. There's a little difference in the printing of the company name at the top, and the numbers there aren't exactly the same, but you'd never notice if you didn't lay them side by side."

"It took Atherton three days to get hold of an engraver and cut the plates," said William. "At that the fellow must have worked night and day."

"And earned himself a pretty penny," said Doc.

"Maybe we should start by roundin' up all the engravers in the territory," suggested Raider.

William shook his head. "I don't see what good that'd do. Even if we found him he wouldn't know where Atherton's gone. Why would he tell him? Tell anybody?"

The marshal restored both certificates to the drawer of his desk and locked it.

"It's crazy," he said. "Mayor Beamon bought ten shares, then ten more for Mrs. Beamon. His were the real thing, hers as phony as my second batch."

"Again, the timing," said William. "The company had the certificates printed. Atherton didn't know what they looked like until they hired the bank to handle the public sale."

"I wonder why he didn't go straight to the engraver who did the company's work and make a deal with him to overprint the issue," said Doc.

"He didn't want to take the chance," said William. "If the fellow refused to go along with the idea he'd probably warn the company. In which case Atherton would go to jail before he could finagle a red cent. No, he needed his own engraver, somebody he could trust."

"Somebody who'd probably done such a thing before," said Doc. "Which would be why he knew he could trust him. Maybe Raider's got an idea. Maybe we should round up engravers, at least the ones with shadowy reputations."

William rejected this, repeating his earlier comment that Atherton would never confide in his engraver, never tell him where he was heading. There'd be no need to do so.

Doc pressed the idea. "He could have inadvertently tipped off his destination."

Raider listened and said nothing. They were reaching for straws, he decided; with nothing concrete to go on they were manufacturing leads out of thin air. Leads themselves so thin they defied grasping. He sat on the windowsill plunging deep into his head, putting himself in Atherton's shiny shoes. A thought came to mind, quite unexpected but interesting. What if Atherton's plan was to get rid of the stock? What if he already had a buyer set? If so he could wash his hands of the whole scheme overnight and be in the clear. When they caught up with him he'd be drowning in money, but they wouldn't be able to find a single incriminating certificate on him. And that was the evidence that would nail him, not money, no matter how much he had. He'd have some phony explanation for the money, and it would be up to the territory to disprove his story, not up to him to prove it. Yes, if he were Atherton the first thing he'd do when he got away safely would be to dump the stock.

Or would he? If he held on to it, in time it could be worth twice, maybe three times as much.

"Smoke..." he muttered. All three turned to him. "We're tryin' to grab smoke. The bucket's empty. We don't even have what with to start with. Marshal, does anybody in this town know anything personal about the man? He was single, lived alone, but did he have relatives? Where'd he come from?"

"Orus Talmadge would know, if anybody," said Rhilander. "They worked elbow to elbow. Orus was the most surprised man in town when the story broke, and he was the one who broke it. Up to then he didn't have an inkling what Atherton was up to, close as they were. Still waters..."

"Let's go see him," said Doc.

The marshal was gazing at them, an appealing expression on his face. "This is some mess. People are up in arms, riding out in bunches looking for Atherton. Every new rumor sends out more. Half the men in town are scouring the territory. They find him, they'll string him up. Bad business ...bad."

• • •

Orus Talmadge was older than Atherton by ten years. He was a handsome man, dark-skinned, suggesting Spanish forebears. His hair was gray, but his beard still had mostly red in it in stubborn defiance of the advancing years. Oldest of all his physical characteristics was his voice—it was worn, tired, and cracked easily when he raised it. He welcomed them into Atherton's office, which he told them he had taken over.

"You want to know about Eustace." He shook his head and his eyes saddened. "He was my friend. I think I was his only friend, at least here, only because we worked so closely together, saw each other every day, sat beside each other in church, dined together. This hasn't been easy, boys.

"He was a very private person. Oh, he was outgoing, especially to the customers, but not really. How shall I say it? He was hail-fellow-well-met, but he drew the line at letting folks meet the real him, the man inside."

"Very well put," said Doc.

"Funny, another fellow was in here not fifteen minutes ago asking about Eustace, his habits, idiosyncrasies, likes and dislikes."

Doc and Raider exchanged glances.

"What'd this fella look like?" Raider asked.

"Older man. Salt-and-pepper fundamentalist beard. Wore thick spectacles. Made his irises big as ripe olives. Spoke with a Southern drawl. Insurance investigator with the company that's insuring the Big Bonanza outfit." He paused and frowned. "At least he said he was an insurance investigator. Come to think of it he didn't show me any business card. Kelsey, he called himself. You boys recognize him?"

"Maybe," said Doc. "Has anybody else been in asking about Mr. Atherton?"

"No."

"Did you see where he headed when he left?" Raider asked.

"No."

"Please tell us what you know about Atherton," said

William. "Everything, no mater how inconsequential you may think it is. We want to get a line on where he may have headed.

"I don't know. I've wracked my brain trying to figure that out. All I can tell you is that he could go anyplace on earth and live royally. He was very well fixed. He lived alone, made a good salary and sound investments, and saved every cent. I guess when the Belinda came along he decided it was his chance to move from comfortably to royally. I'm sure sorry he did it; he was a fine man. I'll miss him."

Atherton had come to Mortality from Montana; Helena, Talmadge thought, but he wasn't certain. He had banking experience; he had gone to work in the bank under then President Wallace. Wallace took an immediate liking to him. Mrs. Wallace was the real power behind the bank. She came from a wealthy family; she organized the bank and installed her husband as president. Both became fond of Atherton.

"Two years after Eustace started working Wallace died suddenly. The day of his funeral his widow named Eustace to replace him. Six months later she died."

Atherton ran the bank intelligently and profitably for the next twelve years. He was particularly skillful at reading individuals as risks for loans. It could be said that he never once misread, a phenomenal record. He knew the business, knew people, and people liked and trusted him. They came from miles around to deal with the bank, and to him in large measure went the credit for its reputation of excellence. Talmadge cited it as the reason the Big Bonanza Company selected the Miners & Merchants Bank as sole disbursing agent for the Belinda stock. Two years before, the Territorial Bankers Association named Atherton banker of the year.

"Did he ever take a vacation?" Doc asked.

"Not that I recall. Never went anywhere. Oh, he'd take a day off now and then, and last year he was confined to bed with the flu for more than a week. I went to see him every night to go over the day's business, keep him up to date. When he got better he went straight back to work. I remember telling him he ought to take time off, get away. He never did. No vacations, not for the fourteen years I've known him."

Raider stood up and stretched. "I'm goin' over and take a look around his place," he said.

"We'll all go after we finish here," said William.

"I'll go now. You don't need three of us here."

William's expression disagreed, but he didn't object. Instead he shrugged and turned back to Talmadge. "Did he have any lady friends?"

"Eustace? You must be kidding. He couldn't be bothered. Oh, he was very pleasant with women, gracious, not a woman-hater, not by a long shot. Just not interested. You've got to understand, banking was his whole life. It was his kingdom, and the bank was his castle."

Raider grunted, got directions to Atherton's house from Talmadge, and left.

Utterby found the back door locked but a rear window open two inches. Upending the rain barrel and standing on it, he was able to push the window fully open and climb inside into the sink. The house was small and badly in need of painting outside and in, but it was tidy. He sensed a woman's touch and made a mental note to check that angle. Housekeepers, even cleaning ladies, were marvelous receptacles for information. They developed their assessment of the people they worked for by their habits around home, by what they used and didn't, how they took care of their things, what they saved, valued, and were fond of. Yes, by all means find out who kept Atherton's house for him and talk to her. She could very well provide information she didn't even realize she had.

He stood in the kitchen and looked about. It didn't make much difference where he started. At that, he didn't even know what to look for. He ran a hand down his luxurious fundamentalist beard and removed his prop spectacles."

"You'll know when you find it, old boy."

He chuckled. The two Pinkertons had been able to track him to Mortality by his careless doodling. Scrawling the word Belinda on his scratch pad had been a wholly unconscious action, however, so how could he be expected to remember doing it? A lot of people doodled. Maybe Atherton did. There was no desk in the parlor, though, and none upstairs in any of the three bedrooms. No permanent writing place. If he did his writing at home at the kitchen or dining room table, which seemed to be the case, there'd be no chance to leave a clue of any sort behind. He searched every drawer in the house in the hope of finding something that had been stuck far back when the drawer was full and consequently was overlooked when emptied. He found not a scrap; Atherton's carefulness was beginning to gall. So tidy, so well organized was Atherton that common sense advised Utterby that if he found one letter he'd find a packet bound with a ribbon. He found none.

"Infuriatingly thorough."

Tintypes or any kind of photograph might prove worthwhile. People kept photos and usually wrote on the back: the name of the person, the date, sometimes the place where the picture was taken. Atherton was close to fifty. Fifty years in the world was ample time to experience many things, accumulate a host of memories, make many friends. Talmadge had mentioned that he'd come to Arizona from Montana, and thought he'd lived in Helena. That was fourteen years ago. Was it possible he'd gone back there? Remotely possible, but Utterby wasn't about to go running off to find out.

He didn't bother to check for secret hiding places. Again common sense advised that if the man hid anything, either valuable or incriminating, he'd hardly leave it behind. It would be the first thing he'd pack or destroy.

He found cold ashes in the fireplace, which struck him as peculiar. The last thing anybody living in Arizona in the heat of summer needed was a fire, and if these ashes were from his last fire of the winter, why hadn't he cleaned them up? Why hadn't his housekeeper?

He knelt and sifted them through his fingers. He uncovered the ash dump trap and lifted it free. Poking inside the trap, all he found was more ashes. He washed his hands at the kitchen pump, then went back upstairs for a second look around.

Raider arrived. He hobbled his horse out front and walked around the house. The kitchen window was wide open, the breeze seizing the chintz curtains and pulling at them playfully. He tried the door, found it locked, and climbed through the window, dragging his wounded leg in after him; in so doing he smashed his kneecap in the bottom of the sink and cursed roundly. When he stood up and ran his hand gently over his knee to soothe it, his pants felt wet. There was water around the sink drain.

"Elmo, you fox you."

Raider was upstairs poking through drawers when Doc and William arrived. He came down and let them in the front door.

"This place is clean. I couldn't find a hair in the plunge bath even."

"We've checked," said William. "He did his own housekeeping."

"Man's neat as a pin. Talmadge tell you anything after I left?"

William shook his head. "Nothing earth-shattering." Doc stood rubbing his chin thoughtfully, his face screwed tightly into a frown. William noticed. "What's bothering you?"

"Orus Talmadge."

"Did I miss something?" William asked.

"It's just a hunch, but it won't seem to go away. How did he strike you two?"

"Why don't you tell us what's on your mind, Doc," said Raider.

"Talmadge said Eustace was a very private person. He also said they worked very closely together. He implied he was Eustace's only friend, or the closest thing to a friend he had."

William nodded. "That's the impression I got."

"Spit it out, Doc. What is it? You think they're in cahoots?"

"What do you think? Think like Eustace. You leave town, you take it for granted people are going to come after you. He knows we will, and he can assume people in town will. Not the marshal—he's got his hands full with the Claggetts and other things—but the investors he burned. Wouldn't it be convenient, wouldn't it be ideal to have a trustworthy accomplice back here keeping watch on things, able to apprise him of everyone's every move?"

"Isn't that a bit fanciful?" William asked.

"Sounds like more bullshit to me," said Raider. "Sounds like you're fittin' a theory to your hope."

"What?"

"Cookin' somethin' up outta thin air again,. If Talmadge is in cahoots with him he's sure stickin' his neck out, hangin' round town. How they supposed to communicate? The Western Union office spot anythin' suspicious comin' in from Atherton or góin' out from Talmadge they'll run straight to the marshal. You know how these things are, everybody turns into a detective."

"I found Talmadge very forthright," said William. "He didn't have much to tell us, but I think he told us all he did know."

"Maybe," said Doc. "I know one thing, though—if he leaves town I'm going to follow him."

"If Elmo does I'll follow *him*," said Raider.

William looked from one to the other. "You two are sure he was the insurance investigator who called on Talmadge?"

"Bet your life on it," said Raider.

Doc nodded.

"Then he's sure to come out here to look around."

"He's already been," said Raider, showing his dampened kneecap. "He used the sink pump."

Doc lit an Old Virginia cheroot and puffed. "Getting back to Talmadge, he still strikes me as suspicious. I know Eustace's having him back here watching what's going on is pretty thin, but I can't help this gut feeling."

"Marshal Rhilander said Talmadge was the most surprised man in town when the truth came out," said William. "And he was the one who uncovered it."

"Who else would?" Doc asked. "He certainly couldn't stand by and let somebody else in the bank go over the figures, examine the stock certificates, any of it. Just now, did he strike either of you as really shocked by it all?"

"He's had plenty of time to get over the initial shock."

"Maybe. Well, shall we?"

William searched upstairs, Raider the kitchen and outside the house. Doc started in the parlor. The ashes drew his attention. They looked as if they'd been gone through. Raider uncovered the cold hole in the kitchen floor. In it he found a head of lettuce, nothing else. He went through the cabinets mounted high on the walls at either end of the kitchen a second time, as well as those above the window over the sink and the ones under it. William found an old suitcase on a closet shelf in one of the bedrooms. It looked to be empty until he ran his hand through the elastic cloth pocket. He found an enameled Masonic emblem charm. Talmadge had not mentioned that Atherton was a Mason, but perhaps he wasn't active locally. Perhaps he chose not to jeopardize his privacy by joining a lodge.

"William," Doc called from downstairs. "Rade."

Raider had wandered outside to look around the house. He came back in and joined Doc with William in the parlor. Doc had found a charred fragment of paper in the rear of the fireplace. His curiosity aroused, he slipped a page torn from a copy of Jacobsen's *Principles of Banking* under the fragment, carefully lifting it out and setting it on the table.

"There's writing on it," he said. "One of you light that banquet lamp on the corner table and bring it over here."

"It's nothin', Doc," grumbled Raider.

William lit the lamp and brought it over. Doc removed

the lace-flounce-trimmed shade. He then gently pushed the scorched fragment to the top of the page and above it until less than an inch of the lower portion remained on the page. Holding it against the page, he lifted the page and positioned the exposed portion so as to catch the full glow of the lamp. The three of them read in chorus.

"August 4th. Mr. Elliot Lyseka, Hampton, Enderby & Lyseka Securities Corporation. Fifty-two Wall Street, New York City, New York."

"Judas Priest!" burst William.

"Good Lord," whispered Doc.

"I don't get it," groused Raider. "Is that who he's doin' business with, do you think? Is that what you think? How could that be? If he's writin' them, and that's what it looks like, how come he didn't send it? If there's a letter it should be addressed to him, shouldn't it? Not the ones he's writin' to. I don't get it."

"Maybe he started this letter and stopped and threw it away for some reason," said William. "And started over on a second one."

"If that's so how come it's not crumpled?" asked Raider. "When you start writin' a letter and quit you don't just throw it away, you crumple it up. I do. Even if he crumpled it up and straightened it out again, maybe to check what he wrote, there'd be crumple lines, wouldn't there? Wouldn't there?"

"He's right," said Doc.

"Maybe he's just not a crumpler," said William.

Raider exhaled with a disapproving sound. "Everybody crumples. So what do we do now, go to New York?"

"I don't see as that's necessary," said William. "Not right away at least. We can wire George Bangs in the New York office, fill him in, and ask him to check this company out. He works with the police department, so he can get their cooperation. He can question this Elliot Lyseka, get a warrant, and go through their files. I think it's a damned fine lead. Good work, Doc."

Raider sniffed but refrained from comment.

"You two contact Bangs," said Doc. "I'd like to go back and talk to Orus Talmadge." William's unenthusiastic expression in response to this caused him to hurry his words. "With the idea in mind that he's Eustace's accomplice. I'll look with different eyes, listen with different ears. It's worth a try."

"You sound like you've found him guilty and the gallows is going up," said William wryly. "Talk to him if you want to. Raider, we'll go back to the hotel and see what luck we have condensing the whole story to wire George."

"I wanna look some more," said Raider. "That thing could pan out nothin'. There could still be a better clue."

"If there is, a dollar'll get you two that Utterby's already found it," said Doc.

"The son of a bitch. He's back to one step ahead of us like before. Son of a bitch is a fox. Come on, Billy, let's look anyhow."

"Back again?"

Orus Talmadge smiled congenially and gestured Doc to a chair. As he had done prior to the first meeting, he leaned out the door, told his secretary he was not to be disturbed, and closed the door.

"A few things occurred to me after we left," said Doc. "For example, did Eustace ever have a housekeeper?"

"To my knowledge, no."

"You said he earned a good salary and saved his money. That he made sound investments. Stocks and bonds?"

"Yes. He dealt with one particular brokerage house in New York City. For years. I don't recall the name."

"Hampton, Enderby, and Lyseka."

Talmadge stared. "That's it."

Doc's heart sank slightly. So Atherton had been dealing with them all along. It was possible the letter had nothing to do with the Big Bonanza stock. Still, it was dated August 4th. Today was the 26th. On second thought, it could very well pertain to that particular stock.

"How did you know?" Talmadge asked.

"Just guessed."

"Funny. But seriously, how *did* you know?"

"We ran across some correspondence when we searched his house. What other investments did he hold?"

Talmadge pulled open a drawer. "There's a list around here somewhere." He searched the drawer, closed it, and started on the one under it. Doc waited patiently, studying his face. His mask of innocence remained intact, if that was what his expression was. He found the list in the bottom drawer.

"Union Pacific, Southern Pacific . . ."

Doc grunted.

"Allied Gold Mines, Wells Fargo, a slew of different bank stocks, Chicago, Detroit, New York."

"That'll do, thank you."

"Would you like a copy of this?"

"No, thanks. What I'd really like, if you don't mind, is to go over this office."

Doc stared at Talmadge as he spoke. And caught him wincing ever so slightly. Not like he'd been stung or even pinched, but rather like he'd felt a slight twinge of discomfort in a muscle. But a wince, nevertheless.

"If you want to. If you think it might be helpful," Talmadge said evenly.

"It could be more helpful than the house. If this is his castle, his office is his throne room. There's no telling what of a personal nature he might have kept here."

"True, true. Why don't you come back around closing time? That way you could stay as late as you please."

Doc's gut feeling rearranged itself, making itself more comfortable in his stomach. Talmadge wanted time to search first; either that or the chance to get rid of something that might be helpful to them. Could it be something that tied him to Eustace? Wouldn't that be lovely!

"I suppose if I asked to search now it would be disruptive."

"Well . . . I do have work to do, and I've an appointment in ten minutes. Customers pop in. You understand."

"I understand."

Talmadge rose from his chair. "Come back at five of six, why don't you? We close at six sharp. You can stay and search to your heart's content."

"I'd appreciate it. You've been very cooperative, Mr. Talmadge."

"Glad to be. Till five of six then. Good day, Mr. Weatherbee."

Doc checked with the desk at the American Hotel, where they had registered. Raider and William had yet to return from Atherton's house. He couldn't imagine they'd find anything else helpful, and in fact, at this stage there was no way of knowing that even the discovery of Hampton, Enderby & Lyseka would be helpful. At the moment, given a choice, he would put his money on Orus Talmadge. There was something in the office he had neglected to remove first chance he got, or he suspected something might be there, or that something he could have overlooked when he first searched came to mind now that could prove informative, embarrassing, incriminating.

"Something, God willing."

He had no intention of going back to search. Better to let Talmadge search for them. He would take up his post across the street from the bank just before six. When Talmadge came out he would accost him and bluntly demand that he hand over what he'd found. Or ask to search him.

"That's fairly heavy-handed, Weatherbee. William might object."

He'd have to think about it. He checked his watch. Ten past five. Raider and William approached on horseback. They waved him greeting and dismounted in front of the Western Union office.

"Find anything else?" Doc asked.

"Nothin'," said Raider. "How'd you do?"

He told them.

"You actually saw him wince when you asked to search the office?" asked William.

"Absolutely. No question about it."

"It probably just upset him," said Raider. "He's probably got nothin' to hide, just doesn't like the idea of a stranger plowin' through his personal stuff."

"If that worried him, why not take a few minutes and search with me right then and there? Can you think of a better way to throw off suspicion?"

"What makes you think anything of Atherton's still there?" asked William. "Talmadge must have cleaned the place out right off the bat, as soon as he was certain Atherton left and wasn't coming back."

Doc remained unconvinced. "Why did he wince? Why put me off till closing time?"

"Smoke," said Raider.

"Oh, shut up!"

William composed a lengthy telegram to George Bangs in New York at the Western Union counter rather than adjourning to the hotel. In it he advised Bangs to contact William Wagner in Chicago for the specifics of the case and whatever details he could provide. Doc watched the clerk count the words and William pay him, but no sooner had he done so then Doc spoke his piece.

"I don't think Hampton, Enderby, and Lyseka is worth a tinker's dam," he said. "I think the answer to our prayers is right here in town. Right across the street in the bank."

"Weatherbee, you blow hot and cold like nobody I ever seen," Raider rasped. "Why don't you make up your mind, for Chrissakes!"

William was eyeing the clerk at his key. Absorbed in transmitting the message, he was paying no attention to them.

"Let's talk outside, boys."

The clerk stopped. "I hope you guys catch up with that snake in the grass. I bought eight shares in that foolish mine. Now all any of us hears is how the silver's jumping out of the veins and Atherton's holding all the stock while we all of us sit stewing and wondering if he'll ever get caught and punished."

"We're doing our best, friend," said William.

"I know something you don't know." He flattened his thinning sandy hair across his scalp with one hand, then the other, licked his lips, and swallowed, sending his prominent Adam's apple down his throat and back up again. He lowered his voice to a conspiratorial whisper and his head with it. The three of them crowded the counter.

"He sent a wire back to Mr. Talmadge."

"Did he?"

William's wide eyes widened further. Triumph brightened Doc's face.

"From where?" asked Raider.

"Kansas City. Came in yesterday around closing time. I delivered it to Mr. Talmadge myself."

"What did it say?"

Up went a finger requesting patience. He went into his copy drawer. "Here it is. Ahem. 'Sorry about this. It's been a rewarding experience working with you. No pun intended. Sorry that we'll never see each other again. Shall miss you. Afraid you won't be hearing from me ever again. Please try and understand and don't judge me too harshly. Your friend.'"

"Lemme see." Raider snatched it from him. "No signature."

"Any idea who it might be from?" asked William, winking at Doc.

Doc was not amused. "Don't be wise." He thanked the clerk and hurried William and Raider out the door. "Beautiful!" he exploded. "Perfect!"

"I don't follow you," said William.

"Talmadge!"

"Maybe I missed something. It sounded perfectly innocent to me. What do you think, Raider? Did you read anything into it that could possibly incriminate Talmadge?"

"Nope."

"Ask yourselves this: why didn't he tell us he heard from him? It strikes me it would be the first thing he'd tell us if he's on the up and up. Is it possible it's in code, something prearranged between the two of them? Shouldn't we go back in there and get an exact copy of it and see if we can figure it out?"

Raider looked past Doc. "Speakin' o' the devil . . ."

Talmadge was trudging toward them all smiles, waving a telegram.

"Mr. Pinkerton, boys, you forgive me. I completely forgot to tell you about this telegram I got from Eustace yesterday. In all the fuss and feathers it completely slipped my mind. Here, read it."

CHAPTER SIXTEEN

More out of courtesy than curiosity, William read Talmadge's telegram, then handed it back and thanked him. They watched him walk back to the bank and inside.

Doc followed him, his eyes narrowed in suspicion. He nodded. "He had to come running with it, you know. It must have suddenly dawned on him that the clerk would have a copy."

"It doesn't implicate him in the thing," said William. "If anything, just the opposite."

"I'm still going back at five of and search that office," said Doc grimly.

"I think you'll be wasting your time, but if you want to . . ."

The door behind them opened; the clerk waved a message. "This just came in for you, Mr. Pinkerton."

William read it and passed it to Doc without comment. Raider read over his partner's shoulder.

REPORT DEMING NM ASAP STOP SP XPRESS
ROBBED 120T STOP OPS SHAW QUIDERO SMALLEY
AWAIT YOU STOP ESH IN NEW LATHER STOP QUICK
ARRESTS THIS CASE CAN ONLY HELP STOP IN-
STRUCT W RESUME DAILY BULLETINS THIS OFFICE
DETAILING PROGRESS MORTALITY SITUATION STOP
ESH INSISTS DEADLINE STANDS

"Well, it was a pleasure working with you boys," said
William airily.

"You lucky dog," groused Raider. "You get off the hook
and leave us with it sharp up our backsides."

"I have the utmost confidence in you both."

Raider was about to comment further when he suddenly
stopped, gawked, and pointed down the street.

"Look! It's him! Utterby!"

The object of his attention, a well-built older man sporting a fundamentalist beard, glasses, a Dakota hat, and a
dark broadcloth suit, was preparing to mount his horse.
Everyone within fifty yards turned to look at Raider in
reaction to his outburst.

"The beard, the specs . . . It's him, Doc!"

This turned the man's head. His face could not be seen
clearly in the shadow of his hat brim, and the lower half
was covered by the beard, but his reaction seemed to com-
bine fear and surprise.

"I'll get him! I'll get him!" shouted Raider.

He hobbled to his horse, which was hitched six steps
away, and vaulted into the saddle. The man heeled his horse
and started off at a gallop. About seventy-five yards sep-
arated them. Doc called to Raider, but he ignored him. He
bent low and pushed his mount into full gallop. His quarry
rode a bay stallion that accelerated surprisingly fast for a
big horse. Raider's mustang boasted plenty of spring, but
if the chase proved long it would tire before the horse ahead
of it.

They pounded south toward Williams. Raider heeled belly,

slapped flanks, and urged the mustang on in a soothing tone, but over the first mile he failed to close the gap; if anything he slipped farther behind by a few yards. Narrow-chested, light-boned, and drooping-rumped, his mount lacked the stamina and endurance of the horse ahead. Utterby stuck to the road, sending up dust in such quantities it all but obscured him. Far ahead a black smudge nudged the horizon. It grew larger, developing corners and a definite shape, and split in two: the Claggett's house and barn.

"Run, horse. Please! Move! The son of a bitch gets to that house and they're home they'll be more'n I can handle. If he gets to the barn . . . You listenin' to me? Move!"

The horse was giving its all, but Utterby was riding for his life, and his horse seemed to know it. It fairly flew. Raider growled in frustration. Closer and closer came the Claggett property. In desperation he drew and fired four times. Through the scrim of dust he barely made out Utterby veering right, then abruptly left. He fired two more shots. Utterby passed an outcropping to his left, swerved off the road, and pulled up.

Time spun backwards: it was the rock Doc and he had crouched behind in the shoot-out earlier. Great cover, only now Utterby had it and he had nothing he could see within a quarter mile in every direction. Only a rain ditch. A shot coming at him followed by two more convinced him that beggars couldn't be choosers. He pulled up and practically threw himself down into the ditch, landing on his bad leg and bellowing in pain. Utterby continued firing. Raider counted to six as he flattened on his side and reloaded. His horse ambled slowly off, wholly indifferent to the action.

Raider spun the cylinder, turned over on his belly, and raised up for a look. There was no sign of man or horse. He waited. Utterby raised up and fired wildly. By the time Raider could answer, his target's hat had dropped from sight, Raider thumbed home two more shells. They began exchanging fire in earnest, neither willing to raise upward long enough to take decent aim. It was stupid, ridiculous, pointless. The one who ran out of cartridges first was the loser.

"Stupid!"

He bellied forward, slipping off his hat and sliding over it. A shot slammed the edge of the ditch to his left not five inches from his face. He froze, shrinking into himself. Utterby couldn't possibly see, but he seemed to sense that Raider had moved forward. He proceeded to empty his gun at the same spot. Raider yelled between the fifth and sixth shots, and held his own fire.

He counted off twenty seconds, enough time for Utterby to reload, then shoved sharply upward and blasting. It worked. Utterby's curiosity tempted him to chance a look. Raider caught him exposed to just below his shoulders, two-handing his gun, gaping questioningly. Raider fired. The shot struck Utterby's gun. He yelled and let go. Down it clattered, coming to rest in the sand, well out of reach.

Raider advanced on Utterby, who stood up, hands high.

"We meet again 'old boy.' Your luck's still holdin', I see; you're lucky I didn't blow your head off."

"Don't shoot."

"Come down here. Come on!" Raider said. Then he fired. The slugs richocheted off the top of the ledge left and right, bracketing Utterby. Down he stumbled, nearly falling, but keeping his hands up.

Raider strode up to him. "You son of a bitch!" Reaching out, he grabbed the beard and yanked it.

Utterby cried out in pain, cursed, and retaliated with a kick in the shins.

Raider howled. "What the hell you doin', man!"

Bent over, the muzzle of his gun pointing straight downward, Raider rubbed his shin gingerly and goggled as the truth came to him.

"You're not him!"

"I haven't the slightest idea who 'him' is, you lunatic. My name is Charles W. Rutherford. I'm a law-abiding citizen, a church deacon..."

"How come you run away?"

Raider could feel embarrassment filling his upper body, rising to his cheeks, setting them glowing. Nothing he could say, no excuse, no apology could correct his horrendous mistake.

"Wouldn't you run?" snarled the man, "if a madman shouted at you and came barreling after you? You are certifiably insane."

"I mistook you for somebody else."

"You nearly killed me. Marshal Rhilander'll hear of this. You should be locked up. It's getting so decent people can't even ride into town without some half-wit attacking them!"

"I'm sorry. Honest."

"You're an idiot! Look at my clothes. They're a disaster, and I just had them cleaned and pressed. You could have broken my horse's leg, or my neck. You could have killed me, you moron! Blithering idiot! Get away from me! Get out of my sight!"

Elmo Utterby had stopped within sight of Williams to removed his thick spectacles and beard and cleanse the makeup from his face. Overhead storm clouds were gathering rapidly, but in his heart the sun burned in all its glory. Reaching into his inside jacket pocket, he brought out a packet of letters, three in all, neatly bound with a white silk ribbon. He smelled them. The lavender scent was barely recognizable. The letters were from a Mrs. Alden Weatherpark—Emily—of El Paso. He had found them behind the bottom drawer of Atherton's bureau in his bedroom. Mrs. Weatherpark had recently lost her husband. She and Atherton had been friends twenty years ago in Helena, Montana. They had been in love, or at least Atherton loved her. He had even proposed marriage. In her letters she did not allude to her reason for turning him down, but she had, and eventually she married Dr. Weatherpark, a local dentist.

But the passing years failed to erase the memory of Eustace Atherton. She called him "Huey." She had had three sons, all grown up, married with families, established, "doing well." She had four grandchildren; she lived alone; she was lonely; she longed to see Huey again.

"El Paso, old boy. By train it shouldn't take more than ten or twelve hours."

Providing he encountered no delays. He restored the letters to his pocket, and as he rose into town, he thought about the Pinkertons. Doc had had the most astonished look on his face when he jumped over the side of the ramp; Raider was livid. Neither could get a hand on him to stop him, thanks to the crowd. Half an hour later he had drawn the rest of his savings out of the bank, $530 and change, and bought his train ticket. He decided to return by a roundabout route, fearing that the Pinkertons would have every stop on the way covered. Why run unnecessary risks? His first stop would be Carson City, Nevada.

With his ticket he bought a *Chronicle*. The story on the Belinda and Atherton's absconding with the genuine stock certificates, the whole sordid enterprise coming to light, was a frightful shock. He recalled how his hands shook, rattling the paper, the sound turning heads as he read. He felt as if the floor of the train station was dropping from under his feet, plunging him into the pit.

Fortunately, despite his safe, circuitous route back, he was able to beat Raider and Doc, though by only a couple of hours.

He knew now he should have gone straight out to Atherton's house to search, instead of calling on Orus Talmadge. He's wasted valuable time doing so, and even worse, he'd tipped his hand to his two pursuers that he was back in town. When they visited Talmadge he'd tell them he'd already had a visitor. Had he gone directly to the house, they wouldn't know he'd even come back. They might suspect, but they wouldn't know for certain.

But now it was all behind him. Ahead was El Paso, Emily Weatherpark, and her reunion with her old flame. Grown heavy over the years, thanks to his fondness for candy, not particularly dashing, not even good-looking, but a decent sort. If one could discount his crime. Utterby couldn't, nor could anybody in Mortality. But she had loved him once, at least enough to remember him and write and ask him to come, implying it would be well worth his while, even going so far in the third letter as to confess that her biggest mistake was turning him down, and blaming im- maturity for it. It was all rather sad: Atherton had spent his whole adult life carrying the torch; she had spent hers, so she claimed, in regret.

Twenty-eight minutes later he boarded his Texas-bound train, confident that he would not be followed.

CHAPTER SEVENTEEN

Not surprisingly, Orus Talmadge offered to help Doc search the office. He had seen William off and gone back to the bank at a quarter to six, rather than wait for five of. Thunder rumbled and lightning split the sky and brightened Mortality and Arizona, and the rains came heavily while they searched.

"I haven't had a chance to clean out the place completely," said Talmadge, "so it is possible we might turn up something."

He was the soul of cooperation, so eager it confirmed Doc's suspicion that he'd gone over the place with the proverbial fine-tooth comb seconds after this visitor was out the door earlier. They checked over the contents of the desk, going so far as to pull out drawers and search behind and under them and their backs. All they found was a key taped to the underside of the right bottom drawer.

Talmadge examined it. "It looks like his front door key, though it's hard to tell. It'd be like him to keep a spare here."

Doc pocketed it.

They searched for nearly an hour, during which the other employees finished for the day and left and the storm increased in fury. Rain battered the office windows and drummed against the roof. Doc wondered what had happened to Raider. Had he caught up with Utterby? Had there been a shoot-out? Had one or the other been hurt? Possibly killed? Good Lord! He really shouldn't worry about Raider; he could take care of himself. In one on one he had few equals.

"Did Eustace keep anything personal in the storeroom?" Doc asked, glancing about the now thoroughly searched office. "A steel box, important papers, perhaps? What about the vault?"

"No," said Talmadge bluntly.

"You mean not that you know of."

"I mean no. He had a rule against any employee taking up vault space with personal valuables, unless they were willing to pay the standard fee. Nobody keeps anything there. It's not very big to begin with. As for the storeroom, all there is is supplies. We can look through both if you like, but I think you'd be wasting your time."

"That's the one luxury we have."

They searched the vault, or rather Talmadge searched it and Doc stood watching. Nothing turned up in either the vault or the storeroom, other than Atherton's umbrella in the latter.

"I guess he left it there and forgot about it," said Talmadge, closing and locking the door as they went out. "Anything else?"

"I guess that does it."

"Listen to that rain. Say, why don't you take the umbrella? I've got my own and a slicker."

"Thanks, I will."

Talmadge suddenly seemed in a rush to get rid of him. There was no other place to search that Doc could think of, other than the tellers' drawers, and he couldn't imagine

Atherton would put anything in them.

"Thanks again, Orus, you've been very cooperative."

"Just not very helpful, eh?"

Doc smiled. It was exactly what he was thinking.

Raider was waiting for him when he returned to their room in the American Hotel. He had taken off his wet things, wrung them out, and stretched them on the floor to dry. He had almost made it back when the storm hit.

"If I coulda run I probably woulda beat it. Had to hobble and got soaked to the skin, goddamn it."

Doc closed the umbrella. He went to the door and shook it out on the hall carpet. "What happened out there?" he asked, cocking his head to one side, plainly anticipating something other than the truth in response.

"He got away."

"Horsefeathers. The day Elmo Utterby could get away from you on a horse hasn't dawned yet and never will. What did happen?" He caught his breath and brightened, leering. "You caught up with him and lo and behold it wasn't Elmo after all. That's it, isn't it? Isn't it?"

"If that's it, whatta ya askin' me isn't it, isn't it for? If you're gonna answer the question yourself, why bother askin' it?"

"That's exactly what happened. Good Lord, how mortifying. You must have felt like an absolute fool. Lucky it didn't wind up in a shoot-out, you might have killed him. I'll bet he read you the riot act!"

"Why don'cha just shut up about what you don't even know about and are wild guessin' and shouldn't even be talkin' about anyway on accounta it's none o' your damned beeswax. I didn't see you chasin' after him."

"I wouldn't have bothered if he asked me to."

"Not much."

"Not at all. It's a question of priorities. Atherton comes first; at this stage at least Utterby's a distant second. You heard Hollenbeck. Oh sure, he bawled long and loud about getting him back. Giving him his just desserts. But given a choice, don't you think he'd take the money first? I do."

"How'd you make out with Talmadge?"

"We searched together high and low for more than an hour." He held out the umbrella. "We found this, and oh yes, a key. He thinks it's to Atherton's house. Speaking of which, I think I'll go back out there and have another go at it."

"Oh bullshit."

"What then?"

"Nothin' then. We can talk about it in the mornin'. I'm wet and hungry and thirsty and bushed. I'm gonna have me a steak as thick as a brick smothered in onions, a whole bottle o' fire, get on a roarin' drunk, go to bed, and sleep the sleep o' the pure."

"Bully. Oh my yes, that poor man must have called you every name in the book when you caught up. When you got him face to face, couldn't you see it wasn't Elmo? Or didn't you bother to look? I wish I could have been there. I'll bet you were crimson with embarrassment."

"Just shut up about it, wouldja? Is Billy gone?"

"You want to change the subject."

"I'm goin' to eat. Do me a favor and find your own place. I'm not about to sit through a whole supper listenin' to you run off at the face."

"I'm sorry, Rade." He fought back a smile. "You did what you thought was right."

"Damn tootin'!"

"How could you know you'd wind up with egg on your face?"

Hour after hour the rain assaulted the windows, turning the street below into a sea of mud. It didn't let up until an hour before sunrise. Shortly after it stopped, Doc awoke. He got up and went to the window. The moon had emerged and the sky had cleared, but it threatened a gray day with little prospect of any sun. He got out the key given him by

Talmadge and sat staring at it and thinking. They had uncovered nothing in the bank that might give a clue to Atherton's destination. Nothing in his house, apart from the
burnt fragment of the letter. Finding it had raised all their
expectations to the extent of seizing on it like a drowning
man grasping at a straw. And pretty much abandoning any
further search. True, after he had left, William and Raider
had stayed on, but how diligently had they searched? Perhaps not very; certainly not very long.

Should he take another crack at the house? He might just
as well; no other course beckoned. He'd love to search
Talmadge's house too. Perhaps they'd get around to it. It
was certainly an angle worth considering. He'd have to think
about it. They needed the man's cooperation. It would be
foolhardy to deliberately antagonize and alienate him.

Still, the gut feeling persisted: something wasn't right
about him, wasn't genuine. He wasn't being as straight-
forward as he wanted them to believe.

"Weatherbee, you do have a suspicious nature. You do
reach for smoke."

Raider sat up. "Whatta ya' doin', talkin' to yourself?"

"I'm going to Atherton's place."

"What for? We already turned it upside down."

"I'll give it one more turn. Get dressed."

"Bullshit. You wanta waste your time, go ahead. Not
me. I'm catchin' me another twenty winks. This bed's com-
fortabler than a pair o' old boots. I like it. I'm not leavin'
it. Have fun."

He rolled over and went back to sleep. Doc tossed the
key up in the air, caught it, and started to wash up.

Sunrise was still a half hour ahead, though from the look
of the sky it still appeared doubtful the sun itself would see
the day. Doc drew up in front of the house. He dismounted
and stood studying it. It looked woefully lonesome, aban-
doned as it was—left to age empty and lifeless until it
collapsed, bringing down its memories. He pictured Ath-

erton with his suitcase packed, taking one last look around, popping a candy into his mouth, pausing at the door and going over in his mind how thoroughly he had covered his tracks, then going out, riding off without looking back.

And Utterby. Where had he gotten to? He'd definitely come back to Mortality. Who could it be but he who had searched the house shortly before they had. And had gone where? Had he found something that would lead him to a specific destination? It did seem likely. If so, Atherton would be in for it.

He climbed the rickety front steps. The key worked. Inside, he went upstairs to begin with the bedrooms. None of them had looked for secret hiding places before. It was agreed then that if Atherton had squirreled away anything that might help them he would have taken it with him or destroyed it in the fireplace. But there was a slender possibility that in cleaning out his "secret place" he had overlooked something. A very slender possibility.

"Smoke, Weatherbee, smoke."

He searched every inch of the bedrooms. He sensed he was becoming discouraged much too early. He took a break, got out an Old Virginia, and went down to the kitchen to pump himself a glass of water. He found a tumbler in an overhead cabinet and was rinsing it, looking out the window, when he spotted something that stopped his breath and started his eyes from his head. He dropped the glass in the sink, jerked open the door, and ran out.

About fifteen feet from the back stoop to the right of the well was a depression, a distinct indentation in the ground the size of a coffin.

"Good Lord! The storm."

He dropped to his knees and began scooping it out. He quickly gave it up and ran back to the house. He searched the broom closet in the kitchen, but there was no shovel, and no tool shed outside. He went back out and resumed digging with his hands. So intent was he on unearthing whatever was buried there that he failed to hear the horse approaching until it was too late. A pistol cracked. The slug whined by his ear. He went rigid.

"Get up."

He did so. He turned. Orus Talmadge sat on a coal black mare with a blazed forehead, a beautiful horse displaying a glossy, meticulously brushed coat, clear dark eyes, clearer even than Talmadge's, which were glaring fiercely at Doc. His gun was pointed straight at Doc's chest. Behind him under the cantle of his saddle a pick and shovel were tied.

"Good morning, Orus."

"You had to come back. You refuse to quit."

"It's my job."

"I have to kill you. I've never killed anybody in my life, except..."

"Eustace."

"That damned rain. When I buried him I couldn't mound the earth; it would have been a dead giveaway. I couldn't come back out while it was raining; I couldn't be sure I'd level it off properly, perfectly, so nobody would notice."

"Don't apologize, you did the best you could."

"Damned rain." He held the gun steady and stared. "You don't understand any of this, do you?"

"I'll try if you put that thing away. It makes me nervous."

"I have to kill you, you know I do. But I have to tell you why. It starts a long time ago. I was going to step into Cedric Wallace's shoes. It was all decided; he told me, promised me. He was a good man, Cedric, his word was his bond. I believed him, why shouldn't I? Only then Eustace came to town. He took Cedric by storm, and Mrs. Wallace, too.

"People like Eustace; he has a knack for making folks like him. It's a gift. I wish I had it. I don't, never did. All I really have to offer is nose to the grindstone. Eustace worked hard too, and they liked him. Cedric and Ethel loved him. He was the son they never had. I was the orphan. He wasn't in town a week before I saw the handwriting on the wall. I wasn't at all surprised when Cedric died and she picked Eustace to succeed him. She invited me to tea. I'll never forget it; she asked me my opinion. Did I think Eustace would make a good president. What was I to say? I didn't say anything, just nodded.

"He was a good president. Twelve years. I know what you're going to ask, why did I stay on when it was all over for me? When I knew my only chance died when she died. Where was I to go? I'd worked in the bank since I was fifteen. And there wasn't a day went by I didn't dream I'd be president. It was all I ever wanted, my dream come true. I never made it. I would have, but along came Eustace."

"Did he know how you felt?"

"We never talked about it. We got along very well. I couldn't very well hold a grudge. Against Ethel maybe, not against him. It wasn't his fault she picked him over me. What hurt most was that she never even thought of me. That was the crusher. All she could see was Eustace."

"When did you find out what he was up to?"

"Early, almost when he started. He was very tidy and methodical. But he made one mistake. He was so eager to count up his certificates he neglected to lock his door. I barged in on him; I was flabbergasted when I found out. He asked me to come in with him on it. He didn't have any choice but to, right? I didn't want to; it rubbed me the wrong way. I haven't spent my whole life in banking, in a position of trust, respected by friends and neighbors, by myself, to destroy it all by turning thief. But I agreed."

"Did he threaten you?"

"No."

"But you agreed."

Talmadge frowned. "You wouldn't have?"

"No."

"I didn't have to do anything. He did it all."

"How much did he steal before he decided it was time to get out?"

"I don't know exactly."

"But you were partners."

It struck a nerve. Talmadge flared. "It was his idea!"

"Of course."

"When he didn't come to work last Tuesday morning I knew something was up. We open at eight. When he didn't show and didn't show I came out here. It was a little after nine. He was all packed and ready to go. When I walked in he had the guiltiest look on his face, like a little boy caught in the jam pot."

"He was going to run out on you."

"I accused him. He pooh-poohed it. 'We made a pact,' he said. 'We're partners. I wouldn't cheat you.' Then he did it. He looked me straight in the eye and said, 'Let's divide up the certificates right now. You get twenty-five percent.' Twenty-five percent, can you imagine? I felt as if a tree had fallen on me. I lost my temper. He tried to calm me down. He did. Then repeated it. Twenty-five percent! When I said I was entitled to half and wouldn't settle for less, that I'd get half or I'd see to it he never set foot out of town, something snapped. He pulled out a gun. Was I surprised! I didn't even know he owned one. He would have killed me in cold blood right there in the middle of the parlor if I hadn't grabbed him. We struggled. He's ten years younger, and stronger, but I was furious. You should have seen me. In a rage. The gun went off. It was deafening. He looked astonished. He tried to speak; blood came out of the corner of his mouth. It was sickening. I was shaking like a leaf."

"What did you do then?"

"The first thing I did was get myself a drink. Then I dragged him out to the kitchen. I don't know why. I guess I thought I could hide him in the cabinets under the sink temporarily. I wasn't about to try to bury him in broad daylight. He wouldn't fit under the sink. It was grisly. I vomited out back. I left him on the kitchen floor and went and cleaned up the blood. I took the certificates and his money, about eight thousand, locked both doors, and went back to the bank. I worked all day. I was very good, not a bit nervous. Well, maybe a little. But it didn't show. I didn't behave suspiciously. It was the longest day of my life. After we closed up I waited till dark, then went back out and buried him."

"What did you do with the certificates?"

"Oh, they're in the vault, every one. Something around eighty thousand shares, preferred and common. And the eighteen thousand cash. It never should have happened, you know. Why did he have to be so greedy? Twenty-five percent. It wasn't a deal, it was an insult. How could he be so unprincipled? It hit me like a sledgehammer. If there was one word, just one to describe him it would have to be principled. That's what Ethel Wallace always said. 'I've never known a man with loftier principles. He's an example to us all.' Some example! He stole from practically everybody in town. It's people like that who give bankers a black eye. He got what he deserved, don't you agree?"

"Who am I to say, Orus?"

"Now I have to kill you."

He looked pained. Doc was suddenly conscious of a drenching sweat. It poured from his armpits; his face and neck were soaked. His skin felt clammy and his heart thundered. The black eye of the gun stared. He could see the rounded ends of the cartridges snug in their chambers.

"I don't want to."

"Nothing personal, right?"

He scowled. "Don't make a joke. It's nothing to joke about. Murder's a terrible thing. The trouble is when you start you can't stop. Understand, I didn't murder him. We were struggling, it went off. Do you want to face me or turn around?"

"If you don't mind, I'll—"

Hoofbeats behind Talmadge. He heard, reacted, and started to turn, holding his aim firm as he did so.

"Drop it, banker!"

He swung the gun around. Raider fired. The bullet slammed into his wrist. He screamed like a woman. Down fell the gun.

"You shot me, you shot me! My wrist! It's broken! Filthy tramp!"

"Oh shut up. You okay, Weatherbee?"

Doc unburdened his lungs of a long, audible sigh. He stood sagging momentarily, then retrieved Talmadge's gun.

Raider dismounted and came forward grinning.

"I saved your life. You gonna thank me or what?"

"Thank you."

"Another five seconds he woulda blown you away." He pointed his gun at the grave. "Atherton?"

Doc nodded. "The stocks are safe in the vault."

"How 'bout that. All this hullabaloo, carryin' on to beat the band, everybody rushin' around like hens with the ax on their tails, and their stocks are safe in the bank vault all the time."

"My wrist is broken," said Talmadge.

"You're lucky I didn't hit you in the face. Pick up your hat and get on your horse. Doc?"

"What?"

"You were in the bank vault, lookin' around. You didn't see the certificates?"

"I . . . wasn't . . . looking for them."

"That's pretty lame."

"Isn't it, though. Shall we go?"

CHAPTER EIGHTEEN

Talmadge's wrist was not broken, only clipped. He directed a savage tirade at Raider for his "cruel and inhuman action" all the way back to town, but reserved the bulk of his anger for Marshal Rhilander. Being caught, wounded, being disgraced were nothing compared to being locked up "like a common criminal" in a cell opposite Virgil and Elon Claggett. He was outraged. He carried on so raucously Virgil threatened to strangle him.

Doc got a telegram off to the chief in Chicago, and one to Hollenbeck. The Southern Pacific would get its $93,000 back with interest, which should please him. Elmo Utterby was still at large, which should refire his resentment toward the Pinkerton National Detective Agency in general and operatives Raider and Weatherbee in particular.

"Good 'nough for the son of a bitch," muttered Raider as they sat over coffee in the Mortality Diner next door to the American Hotel. "I hope we never catch Elmo."

"Don't be ridiculous, you know we have to. At least try."

"Why? Talmadge's gettin' caught puts him outta the money he stole. The poor bastard's out chasin' after Atherton, not even knowin' he's dead and buried. Talmadge is the one we oughta be worryin' about. When all o' them out searchin' for Atherton come back and find out Talmadge is the real devil o' the piece they're liable to storm the poky, haul him out, and string him up."

"That's Evan Rhilander's problem, not ours." Doc clucked and shook his head. "Though it might help Talmadge when everybody gets their money back. I did tell you I was suspicious of him from the first."

"Oh bull! You tryin' to tell me you knew all along he did away with Atherton and took over the operation himself? You tryin' to tell me that? You didn't suspect any such thing, all you had was woman's intuition."

"I beg your pardon."

"You may have suspected he was up to somethin', but you figured Atherton left town as much as Billy, me, and everybody else."

"That wire Orus faked from Kansas City was a nice touch. Even more clever, pretending he forgot about it."

"It was all luck. If it hadn'ta rained last night we'd still be buttin' our heads against the wall, Talmadge'd still be runnin' the show at the bank lookin' like butter wouldn't melt in his mouth, we'd be back and forth with George Banks in New York hopin' for some kinda payoff there, some threat to reel in. Luck, pure luck."

"That's true. Now all we have to do is find Utterby again."

"He's halfway to Guatamala by now."

"I doubt it. It stands to reason he's heading to where he thinks Atherton's gone. Look." The counterman had gone down to the front window and was removing Atherton's wanted poster. "We should get Utterby's printed up and distributed. We may not have a photograph of him, but we can certainly tell an artist what he looks like."

"Don't bother. He'll be in one o' his getups so's his own

mother wouldn't recognize him. Can I tell you somethin'? I like him gettin' away. I like it on accounta I know how much it galls Hollenbeck. You didn't see it gallin' that other fella . . ."

"J. B. Cantor."

"Didn't bother him, but it 'furiated Hollenbeck. That's good, I like it. I say let's forget Utterby."

"That's a very unprofessional attitude."

Raider flicked a fly from the rim of his coffee and raised his cup. "Elmo, old boy, wherever you are, good luck. Have yourself a good life, don't look back, don't get caught."

The door opened. It was the Western Union clerk. He waved a telegram. "Mr. Weatherbee."

Doc tore it open.

> FIND UTTERBY FIND UTTERBY FIND UTTERBY FIND
> UTTERBY FIND UTTERBY FIND UTTERBY FIND UT-
> TERBY FIND UTTERBY FIND UTTERBY FIND UT-
> TERBY FIND UTTERBY FIND UTTERBY
>   ESH

He handed it to Raider. He read it, chuckled evilly, crumpled it, and dropped it on the floor.

"Find him yourself, Mr. Hot Collar."

CHAPTER NINETEEN

Elmo Utterby got off the El Paso & Southeastern train in El Paso travel weary, hungry, and thirsty, but eager for the impending confrontation with the man who had bilked him. He carried a gun. Using it would be a last resort, but its presence in his belt out of sight under his jacket was reassuring. And quite practical; Atherton would be carrying one.

He counted one important edge in his favor. Atherton had never seen him without a disguise; there was no way he could recognize him. With this in mind he resolved to go straight to Mrs. Weatherpark's house, knock on the door, and accost him. Atherton wouldn't raise a fuss in front of the lady. What he would most likely do would be to ask to speak privately with him, and when he got him alone...

"I'll demand he return my stock."

He had thousands of shares, he wouldn't bridle at giving up a mere 1,800, not with the threat of exposure in front of her threatening. All things considered, he anticipated no grave problems. If things went smoothly he could be on the next train out.

He looked forward to meeting Emily Weatherpark. On the long ride down he had passed the time reading and rereading her letters and conjuring up the picture of a lady of delicacy and refinement. Giving his imagination free rein, he envisioned her as beautiful. Meeting her promised a delightful experience. At the same time he envied Atherton. After what he'd done he didn't deserve her; if she only knew she'd throw him over like a tub of rubbish. But he wouldn't be the one to tell her. That would be malicious, and would hurt her as much as it did Atherton.

The day was clear, mild, and dry. The town had recently gained a reputation as a health resort, particularly for sufferers of pulmonary complaints. Situated as it was on the border, it carried on a brisk trade with neighboring Mexico, importing ore, sugar, cigars, and oranges; exporting wheat, boots and shoes, mining machinery, cement, lime, lumber, even beer. Prominent among its factories were railway car shops, and just outside of town there were lead smeltering works.

Mrs. Weatherpark lived in a tidy-looking, freshly painted cottage at the northern edge of town. It appeared out of place among the other, larger homes. A white picket fence surrounded it, and yellow roses climbed trellises concealing the veranda at either side of the front door.

He straightened his tie, squared his shoulders, smoothed his hair, and approached the door.

"Here I come, Eustace, old boy."

She answered his second knock. She was petite, his favorite size in ladies. She wore a navy blue bolero style serge cheviot suit, the outer jacket trimmed all around with black mohair and silk. Her smile caused his heart to skip one, then another beat. He returned her smile, removed his hat, and bowed slightly.

"Yes?"

"Mrs. Weatherpark? My name is George Watson. I'm a friend of Eustace Atherton's."

The name obviously pleased her. "Come in, come in."

The parlor was tastefully furnished and immaculate. The scent of freshly baked bread came wafting from the kitchen. The sun streaming through the side windows lent the interior a golden look. It was so bright, so cheerful, such a welcome ambience after so many dreary hours on the train. On the walls were framed programs from well-known plays, and photographs of famous actors and actresses: Joseph Jefferson as Hamlet, John Brougham as Sir Lucius O'Trigger in *The Rivals*, Anna Cora Mowatt as Rosalind in *As You Like It*.

She offered him a chair. He sat with his hat in his lap, his makeup case on one side, his bag on the other.

"I'm afraid Eustace isn't here."

"Oh?"

"He's coming. He should be here sometime today. You're welcome to wait."

"I wouldn't want to be a bother."

"No bother, really. We can wait together."

She laughed lightly. It was like a small bell. Beautiful. She was. Her eyes were large and warm, capable of expressing enormous affection, he decided. Her small nose turned up slightly, and her mouth was lovely, perfectly complementing her other features. She had to be in her mid-forties, but looked barely more than thirty. Her complexion was as smooth as a young girl's. She wore her auburn hair in a mass of ringlets, and when she sat down opposite him the sun struck it at just the right angle. She looked more goddess than human, one of those lucky individuals whom Nature cannot lavish too many favors on.

What a lucky man Atherton was, he thought, to get this second chance at happiness. He did envy him. It seemed outrageously unfair. She was much too good for him, though she obviously didn't think so. Lucky, lucky fellow.

"Are you in banking too?"

"Finance. I invest other people's money."

"Sounds interesting. Do you travel widely?"

"I have lately."

"And you've worked with Huey in Mortality?"

"Yes."

"Isn't he a fine man? So very bright and hardworking. I'm not surprised he became president of the bank. He was always a go-getter."

"Oh yes."

"It's been such a long time..." Her voice trailed off, and a look of longing crept into her eyes.

"You did say he's coming today."

"He wired he was coming yesterday. It's such a long way; perhaps he was detained. I'm not worried. I'm not a worrier. Huey always called me a blind optimist. He'll be here. He said he was coming, and he will. Does he know you were coming to El Paso?"

"No."

"My, won't he be surprised. Are you here on business?"

"Yes."

He couldn't take his eyes off her. He'd never felt so about any woman; he was prickly all over. He could feel his cheeks burning; he hoped they weren't too red. Every word she uttered drew his heart closer to her. He wanted to reach out and grasp her hands, squeeze them, but of course he couldn't do such a thing. What would she think of him! Yes, a goddess. Truly!

His heart threatened to shatter the wall of his chest. If only he could swallow without showing it. If he held his hand straight out he'd never be able to keep it still. It would tremble off his wrist. She spoke with her eyes directed at her hands in her lap; when she raised them to gaze into his, his upper body began to ache across his chest. He was having trouble breathing. Would that he might dive into those magnificent, mesmerizing eyes, submerge himself in their depths.

His staring didn't seem to make her self-conscious or nervous. Was he succeeding in concealing the effect she was having on him, or was she ignoring it to spare him embarrassment? The Tennessee marble clock with its gilt ornamentation on the mantel ticked on. His heart thudded accompaniment. The sunshine was making him drowsy. She talked on about Atherton. She was dying to see him again "after all these years." If the door opened and he walked in she'd be in absolute heaven. True to her words, she didn't seem worried over his tardiness; impatient with waiting, perhaps, but not worried.

A cold thought pierced his mind. Was Atherton coming as his telegram promised or had he changed his mind? Had something happened to change it? Had the Pinkertons caught up with him? Had he been held up, robbed, murdered? Along with the certificates, he'd surely be carrying a substantial amount of money—fleeing as he was, likely his entire savings.

"Is something wrong?" she asked.

"No, I was just wondering about him."

"You're worried. That's a true friend." She laughed: again it was like a bell. "You must think me giddy because I don't worry. I promise you he'll be here."

The clock struck three. He checked his watch against it. Three on the dot. He glanced about the room.

"I see you're interested in the theater."

"I'm mad about it. We have a theater group here in town and I . . . I try."

"I'm fond of it myself."

"Are you really?"

They began chattering away, each supplying the other with squibs of information about plays and actors, each asking about the other's experiences. They could have talked for hours, but she suddenly stopped.

"Mercy, where are my manners? Here I sit babbling and haven't even offered you tea. It's hot on the stove waiting for Huey. If he's much later I can always brew another pot. He likes Gunpowder. We used to sit and talk and drink cup after cup in the old days. We were great talkers, Huey and I. Let's have tea. Would you excuse me?"

The taffeta under her skirt rustled loudly as she went into the kitchen. He leaned back in his chair. What a perfectly lovely day. What a lovely place. What a lovely person she was.

Oh my yes, Eustace was a lucky fellow.

J.D. HARDEN

**"THE MOST EXCITING
WESTERN WRITER SINCE
LOUIS L'AMOUR"
—JAKE LOGAN**

___ 06572-3	DEATH LODE #14	$2.25
___ 06412-3	BOUNTY HUNTER #31	$2.50
___ 07700-4	CARNIVAL OF DEATH #33	$2.50
___ 08013-7	THE WYOMING SPECIAL #35	$2.50
___ 07257-6	SAN JUAN SHOOTOUT #37	$2.50
___ 07259-2	THE PECOS DOLLARS #38	$2.50
___ 07114-6	THE VENGEANCE VALLEY #39	$2.75
___ 07386-6	COLORADO SILVER QUEEN #44	$2.50
___ 07790-X	THE BUFFALO SOLDIER #45	$2.50
___ 07785-3	THE GREAT JEWEL ROBBERY #46	$2.50
___ 07789-6	THE COCHISE COUNTY WAR #47	$2.50
___ 07974-0	THE COLORADO STING #50	$2.50
___ 08032-3	HELL'S BELLE #51	$2.50
___ 08088-9	THE CATTLETOWN WAR #52	$2.50
___ 08669-0	THE TINCUP RAILROAD WAR #55	$2.50
___ 07969-4	CARSON CITY COLT #56	$2.50
___ 08743-3	THE LONGEST MANHUNT #59	$2.50
___ 08774-3	THE NORTHLAND MARAUDERS #60	$2.50
___ 08792-1	BLOOD IN THE BIG HATCHETS #61	$2.50
___ 09089-2	THE GENTLEMAN BRAWLER #62	$2.50
___ 09112-0	MURDER ON THE RAILS #63	$2.50
___ 09300-X	IRON TRAIL TO DEATH #64	$2.50
___ 09213-5	HELL IN THE PALO DURO #65	$2.50
___ 09343-3	THE ALAMO TREASURE #66	$2.50
___ 09396-4	BREWER'S WAR #67	$2.50
___ 09480-4	THE SWINDLER'S TRAIL #68	$2.50